CHRISTMAS EVE CARNAGE

JOHN LYNCH

For Britney, El, William, and Ronan

It's Christmas. Nothing bad is going to happen on Christmas!

KRAMPUS-2015

A SMALL NOTE

Christmas Eve Carnage is a stand alone title. That being said, the prologue contains references to my short story, The Christmas Tree Farm. It is not required reading, but will allow you to have a better grasp on "who" Santa is, and what happened to him that made him become Santa. I've included that story in the back of the book. I hope you enjoy this gory Christmas tale.

Merrily,

John Lynch

PROLOGUE

Justin Pitts sat on a massive throne upholstered in red velvet. A large, ornamental piece adorned with gold accents, swooping designs, and a back that extended several feet over his head. The smell of gingerbread was in the air, overpowering everything else, even the bourbon in his eggnog—which these days contained far more bourbon than nog. How he loathed the smell of those fucking cookies. There was a time, years ago, when the scent brought him joy. In those days, everything about the Christmas season brought him joy. But those days were long gone, no more than a distant memory.

The Christmas-loving Justin Pitts died years ago. An incident in a tree farm took the last remnants of humanity from him the Marine Corps hadn't. Attacked by mutant elves and a murderous real-life Santa Claus, they'd tried to kill him. Almost *had* killed him. But you know what they say about almost—it only counts in horseshoes and hand grenades.

They'd failed in killing him, but they'd succeeded in sucking the joy out of Christmas. With luck, he'd not only survived that night but had also slain Kris Kringle himself.

He knew it had been luck because once he'd thrown on

the suit, he'd been gifted the title of Santa. And being *the* Santa came with gifts. It came with powers. Powers typically used to spread joy and wonder to all the good little boys and girls. But somewhere along the line the previous Santa had grown tired of Christmas. The magic of Christmas, once joyous and wonderful, had turned dark and malevolent. Santa used those powers to tinker with his elves, transform his reindeer.

Each year, Christmas became more about commercialization, and while the people of Earth made a mockery of the holiday, Santa made a mockery of the holiday's sacred symbols.

But at one point, he became complacent. A fat, lazy, miserable man. That was how Pitts had been able to best the once great Kris Kringle. Not because of skill or his combat training, but because the man had simply underestimated him. Or maybe it was because he no longer cared. Maybe he'd given up. Pitts could see it either way.

Either way, he'd escaped the tree farm with his life and newfound powers.

What life? he thought. *What kind of life is this? Watching these sniveling little shits terrorize their friends, parents, and teachers all year long, only to switch it up and act* nice *for one month a year, all so they can receive gifts they don't deserve. Fuck them, I'm done.*

He understood now why Kris had turned sour. It took time for Pitts to come around; even if that night had taken his love for the season, he hadn't detested it until year after year, he dealt with the same bullshit that had driven the previous Santa insane.

He knocked back the rest of his bourbon nog and threw the glass into the fireplace, shattering it. The jagged pieces sprinkled the firebox, resting on and around the bloodied corpse of the newly deceased Mrs. Claus. Her blood stained the interior of the fireplace, running in between the bricks.

A streak of the crimson, Christmas-colored life essence formed a trail from the middle of the throne room to where the pieces of her now rested. He'd really done a number on her. Severed limbs, flayed skin, decapitated head. But that hadn't been enough—he'd even popped the eyeballs out of their respective sockets and skull fucked her disembodied head.

Pitts's cock grew hard again while he relived the memory. And while the thought of it excited him, he deeply regretted having killed her in the first place. She hadn't deserved it, same as the previous two Mrs. Clauses he'd killed didn't deserve their fates either. But this one? She had been a real beauty. From the moment she'd taken up the mantle of Mrs. Claus she'd done everything he asked and did it with pride. So much so, there was a small part of him that almost found joy in Christmas again, but it was short-lived because soon Santa turned mean to his wife as he had to his previous wives.

Despite this, Mrs. Claus had aimed to please her husband. She'd done an admiral job, ensuring the workshop was clean, the elves stayed on track, and the reindeer were good to go. But then she made a fatal mistake.

Mrs. Claus baked gingerbread cookies. The *one* fucking thing he'd asked her *not* to do. The smell set him off. A mixture of war from his days as a Marine and lingering mental trauma from that day at the tree farm left him with severe PTSD. And Justin Pitts, the new Santa Claus, had a short fuse.

Thinking about his dead wife naturally brought on thoughts of her generous features. She had been quite pleasing to the eye. A thick, curvaceous body—breasts, hips, ass—she had it all. And he'd tossed her away like nothing because of his temper. Where would he find another woman like her? She really had been the total package. Personality, brains, looks. His anger swelled once more—this time at his own stupidity—and he erupted off the throne, storming toward the operations room.

Kicking the saloon doors open, Santa entered the room furious. The mutant elves all jumped, startled at the unexpected intrusion. They were toiling away at their workstations, crafting implements of chaos. Gone were the days of dolls and trucks. Santa had transformed the workshop this year and now they made weapons and morbid toys. Candy cane spears, footballs filled with shrapnel that exploded upon contact, toy guns that shot foam darts—but where the tips had once been plastic caps, now they were poison-tipped needles. No doubt Christmas this year would be one for the books.

Santa made straight for the podium in the center of the room. Past the two-headed skeletal reindeer, past the elves who were now standing ramrod straight, hands raised in a salute with razor-tipped fingers rigid against their brows. They smiled, showing rows of sharp fangs.

Their master was about to ruin some poor child's holiday and the excitement was too much for them to handle; they struggled to maintain their composure.

Santa practically leapt up the three steps of the elevated platform, reaching the podium in the center in a few strides. He stopped in front of it, gripped the edges. The sound of his teeth grinding was loud in his own head. "Bring me the book," he said.

Four elves rushed to the side of the room and stopped before a large glass case. They opened the locked door and removed the massive tome housed inside: the *Naughty or Nice List*. It was heavy but they managed to carry it—two mutant elves on each side—to the podium where Santa waited.

They struggled to place the tome perfectly—it was far too tall, and they were far too short. Their stubby little arms couldn't reach the edge of the podium.

"Useless creatures," he said, snapping his fingers.

The tome rose by itself, Santa's magic ripping it from their grubby little hands. It floated up above the podium, centering itself before dropping into place. A loud thud echoed in the room and a plume of dust shot up, spreading through the air.

Santa coughed, choking on the dust. He opened the cover and flipped page after page, studying the names. Searching for the right child. He didn't know who he would choose, though he knew every child on the planet. But when he found the right one, he'd know. It would be a feeling in his gut.

The elves watched, their breath held tightly in their chests as they waited for Santa to choose the right child.

At last, after what felt like hours—though only a few minutes had passed—Santa's finger stopped on a name.

Cindy Feltcher – Nice.

With a snap of his fingers and a wiggle of his nose, Cindy's name burst into flames on the page. It flickered brightly, and as quickly as it had erupted, the flames sputtered out.

The page remained as pristine as it had been before it ignited, the only blemish—a scorch mark where Cindy's name had once been inscribed.

CHAPTER ONE

Cindy Feltcher walked along the side of the road, bundled up from head to toe. She wore a puffy pink jacket, a knitted cap with a pom-pom on top, and a giant pink scarf that was much too big for her, but it had been her mother's and she refused to wear any other scarf. She didn't care that it had long ago seen its best days, it was *her* scarf. In each hand she carried a plastic grocery bag containing books she'd gotten from the book fair. While most of her class didn't bother with it, Cindy loved the event and usually begged her father for plenty of cash the week leading up to it. Her haul was double bagged but the spines and corners already poked through, threatening to send the precious cargo tumbling into the snow.

Cindy regretted her decision to walk home today. She could have taken the bus with her brother, Adam, or gotten a ride from her sister, Katy, but stupidly chose neither. For Cindy, the holiday season was a special time and this year, her hometown of Glenwood had been transformed into a picturesque winter wonderland. Something you'd see on a postcard or in a Hallmark movie. She wanted to stroll through it like one of the characters in one of those movies and forget about the pain and hurt that life had dealt their family lately.

The blizzard had been a big one. Not like the blizzard of '78, nothing had been *that* catastrophic in the state of Rhode Island since that storm, but enough snow had accumulated that school had been canceled for a few days. And now, a week later, there was still shin-high snow in most of the yards on her walk home. Even better, there was another storm on the way. She regretted taking her schoolwork home for the break, wished she'd stuck her book fair books inside her backpack instead.

After trudging through the snow drifts, wind whipping miniature frozen flecks of snow at her face like microscopic daggers, Cindy arrived home. She stood on the walkway smiling. Dad had put the decorations up, just as he'd promised. That in and of itself was a surprise; the man rarely did household chores. In years past, decorating the house for Christmas was a task her mother had handled. That was until cancer had robbed her from Cindy. She'd fought a long and vicious battle, and though Courtney Feltcher had eventually lost, she'd fought admirably. The medical team had told everyone her outlook was grim but she'd fought so hard, everyone thought she had beaten the odds.

But she hadn't. Cancer didn't care how hard you fought. It was a monster.

After her mother passed, Cindy's father lost himself in work. Sixteen-hour shifts six, sometimes seven days a week. Often even pulling quadruple shifts—thirty-two hours in a row! There was a time not long ago when she resented her father for the hours he spent at work. How could he leave his kids at home to grieve their mother by themselves when they needed their father around to help pick up the pieces?

That was until Katy had explained to her what was really going on. Or at least their father's version of what was going on. Katy said it was a crock of shit, but to Cindy, Jack Feltcher's explanation made sense. He blamed it on the economy and inflation. Before their mother had passed, the economy had crumbled and they were living paycheck to paycheck. But now, with her gone, the responsibility of paying for a family of four fell solely on his shoulders. It was a situation that left him with two options, neither of which he was a fan of. One, greatly reduce their spending, which would mean no more nice things, no more vacations, while continuing to live paycheck to paycheck just to keep food on the table and bills current. *Or,* he could work the extra shifts which would allow them to not only keep the bills paid and their bellies full, but it meant they would live comfortably and not have to worry. And as a bonus, he'd said, he wouldn't feel like he was letting his children down.

There were times when Cindy wished he'd say fuck it, forget about money, and be home with the family. They didn't always have to have the newest technology and go on yearly trips. Plenty of families didn't have those luxuries and were perfectly fine. But there was also the selfish part of her. The *human.* Materialistic, self-conscious. That part of her didn't want to show up to school wearing old clothes, or be caught with an old or cheap model cell phone. Cindy didn't want people at school to think she was poor. Deep down, Cindy knew there wasn't anything wrong with being poor. It didn't make you less of a person or make you a bad person, but it *did* make you a target.

Cindy was both thankful and guilty about her feelings and how much her dad worked to buy her those things that made her feel better. It broke her heart to see him come home from those thirty-two-hour shifts looking like a walking corpse. A broken and battered husk of a human. There used to be a spark in her father's eyes. Now they were hollow and dull, his cheeks gaunt and pale from a horrible diet and lack of sleep. And he did it all for his children.

But despite how much her father was gone, he'd come

through this time. In their yard was a magnificent Christmas display spanning from the front lawn to the rear of the house. Big inflatable reindeer, holiday elves, snowmen. Everything you could think of was there. He must have spent weeks using his lunch breaks at work to speed off to Home Depot and Lowe's in order to buy all of these decorations. Had he returned home to set up the display this morning after he'd dropped her off at school?

Cindy's cheeks warmed, her heart swelled with joy and a sense of pride for her father. She loved him. For as much as she missed him and would complain about his absence, he still did the best he could to keep his children happy.

Smiling, she took in the view as she walked toward her home. Once she'd reached the front door, Cindy placed her bags on the ground and rooted around in her pockets, searching for her keys. For a moment, Cindy worried she had left them at school, but she eventually found them in the front pouch of her backpack. She opened the door and let herself in, the warm air inside further lifting her spirits after walking home in the cold.

Cindy was in a good mood, feeling happy and festive. Dad was supposed to be home a few hours early tonight, so maybe she'd surprise him and bake a few dozen of his favorite holiday snack: gingerbread cookies.

The whole Feltcher house was infused with the aroma of Christmas baking, lending a cozy ambience that Cindy otherwise wouldn't have felt from the empty house.

Neither Adam nor Katy had returned home for the evening yet. Adam was at a friend's house, allegedly doing homework. Katy was at work—the local pizza spot, Tony's Pizza Palace. It seemed as if there were a million pizza joints named Tony's Pizza across the state of Rhode Island. There were three in the town of Glenwood alone! But there was only *one* Tony's Pizza Palace. Cindy felt jealous that her sister was old enough to work. It must be heaven to be around pizza all day. *She'll be lucky if she doesn't gain ten pounds,* Cindy thought, making herself giggle.

Cookie crumbs slipped from her mouth, falling onto the TV dinner tray she had set up on her lap. She'd made herself a dozen chocolate chip cookies after finishing the gingerbread ones for her father. He might love them, but she couldn't stand the damn things. They had a captivating scent, but the taste was abhorrent. Why would anyone choose to eat such a terrible cookie when there were so many better choices out there?

Breaking another cookie in half, she dipped it in a glass of milk. The glass was filled almost to the brim, and the cookie pushed it to the edge. But Cindy had been prepared and kept a napkin under the glass for this exact scenario. Of course it would be easier to simply use less milk, but part of the experience was having enough milk left over to chug when the cookies had been devoured.

Outside, Cindy heard the wind howling. Goose bumps raised on her arms, and the tiny hairs on her neck stood at attention. *I wish someone else was home right now.*

Pushing her tray aside, she crossed the living room and tugged the string hanging from the blinds, shutting them. She couldn't help but feel a sense of unease as she listened to the wind's piercing cries and stared into the abyss of darkness outside. While she didn't fear the dark or the monsters that children believed dwelled within, she was still a twelve-year-old girl with a vibrant imagination. Being home alone didn't help matters.

Cindy decided to head downstairs to the newly finished basement and watch Christmas movies. With the recent work her father had done to it, it wasn't scary at all like many basements. The room was the most inviting in the house, with a large OLED screen television and a fake fireplace insert that mimicked the real deal.

She picked her plate and glass up from the tray and brought them to the kitchen, rinsing both of them before placing them in the dishwasher. Another luxury purchased with Dad's overtime. Adam and Katy couldn't be relied on to wash the dishes—he was too lazy, and she was too busy—so the task had originally landed in Cindy's lap once her mother had passed. But after a few days of poorly washed kitchenware—cups with residue stuck on the bottom of them, plates with flecks of food still crusted to them, a rancid stench in the sink—Jack Feltcher said fuck it and bought the new appliance. He certainly wasn't going to wash the dishes himself, not after spending sixteen hours a day working in a prison.

She closed the dishwasher and made her way back to the couch, snatching the warmest throw blanket she could find from the wicker basket next to the oversized sectional. Cindy draped it around herself like a cloak and made her way out of the living room, back into the kitchen, and toward the basement stairs in the back of the house. As she was about to open the basement door, a muffled noise from upstairs startled her.

What was that noise? Adam isn't home yet, and Katy isn't either . . . but nobody could be in the house, right?

Straining her ears, Cindy attempted to detect unfamiliar sounds, but the silence remained unbroken aside from the initial noise. She wondered if she'd simply imagined the sound.

"You're creeping yourself out again, Cindy," she said.

Cindy turned the doorknob . . . *Thud!*

Again. This time, there was no mistaking it. None of her family had come home yet, but she knew the house had to be empty too. If someone had gotten inside, the perimeter lights would have come on, or the security camera would have sent an alert. *Something* to indicate the presence of another person. But nothing of the sort had happened. Just the mystery noise.

Must be Jonesy, she thought.

Jonesy was a massive, ginger American Shorthair cat. Dad had named him after the cat from *Aliens* because they were practically indistinguishable. For the longest time, Cindy had wondered about the other Jonesy. Her father refused to let her watch the movie, said it would give her nightmares, so she was forced to take his word for it. One evening, she had pestered Adam relentlessly to allow her to watch the movie until he finally gave in. Just as she was about to throw in the towel, he'd reconsidered and grinned. "Okay," he'd said, "I'll show you the movie. But you'd better not snitch and tell Dad."

But Dad *had* found out. Because after watching the movie, she'd been so terrified of the creatures she was unable to sleep alone for weeks. He was livid at Adam, screaming and cursing for what had seemed like ages, but in actuality, had probably only been a few minutes.

Dad had a short fuse, and though he'd never laid hands on his children in anger, he'd certainly given them plenty of verbal lashings. Adam had put on a show, pretending to be upset, but later that evening he'd laughed and admitted the crime was worth the time.

Cindy crept her way back through the kitchen to the front of the house before slowly making her way to the second floor. She would take Jonesy downstairs with her so he couldn't make any more noise. Hopefully, nothing else would give her a fright. Making her way through most of the second floor, Jonesy was nowhere to be found. The only place she'd yet to check was her own bedroom—Jonesy hated the cold and it was far and away the chilliest room in the house.

The large, walk-in attic connected to Cindy's bedroom caused a noticeable temperature difference, making it colder than the rest of the house. Dad had planned to insulate the entire thing this year but the company he'd contracted to do it ended up canceling at the last minute. Like most companies, they were short-staffed and simply had too large a workload. They'd given an option to reschedule for the summer, but Dad was already pissed off about it and instead asked for his deposit back. He was old school, and missing a deadline was unacceptable to him.

She popped her head into her bedroom, giving it a cursory glance—still no cat. Just her bright pink walls, princess bed, and legion of stuffies lined up at the foot of her bed. And every other surface with enough room for them to rest on.

The mystery noise left her stumped. If she'd have found Jonesy at least she might have been able to shake the heebie-jeebies. Instead, she'd have to text Adam and ask him to come home. She'd be forced to admit being a chicken, but admitting to being a chicken was better than being petrified for the rest of the night. Adam, of course, would give her grief about it, but she thought he'd understand. He'd been her age once. Not to mention, she never bothered her siblings to come home and quell her fears. This was the first, and hopefully the last time it would happen.

As she turned around to leave her bedroom, a powerful wind picked up outside. The breeze whisked its way through the gable vent and into the attic. The gust was strong enough to make it down the attic stairs and push the door open, another reason the attic ventilation needed to be updated.

This wasn't the first time the door creaked open like something out of a scary move. One night, when Cindy was much younger, she had been sound asleep in her bed when a tropical storm had passed through Glenwood. Much like tonight, the draft from the attic pushed open the door, frightening her so badly she'd pissed in her pajamas, despite being well past the age for such a thing to be acceptable.

Her bloodcurdling scream caused both of her parents to burst into the room, looks of abject terror etched on their faces. Once they'd realized what had happened, Dad laughed, which earned a punch in the shoulder from Mom. She'd whispered something in his ear, causing him to quickly change his tune. He sat on the bed next to her and explained attic vents and cross breezes. It made sense, as much as it could in her young mind, and she'd calmed down. Still, sometimes her nerves got the best of her.

Cindy was determined not to let this be one of those times. Recalling the memory made her feel foolish.

Today, she would not act like a baby.

Today, she was going to act like the preteen she was, mere months away from her thirteenth birthday. She would not let the wind get the best of her. The more she psyched herself up, the better she felt.

The matter was settled. She would close the attic door, thus proving to herself she was brave. With the door closed, she would then go downstairs and binge-watch Christmas movies until she passed out, leaving her older siblings out of the picture.

With a renewed sense of confidence, Cindy crossed her bedroom in a few swift steps. She felt empowered, two feet taller. At the door, she placed her fingertips against the heavy wood, slowly pushing it closed.

Before the door clicked shut, she heard another thump and a jingling noise, like a small bell. It had definitely come from the attic.

"What the hell is Jonesy doing in the attic?"

Cindy swung the door open and climbed the stairs, calling for the cat. "Here, Jonesy! Here, kitty kitty kitty."

Like all respectable cats, Jonesy didn't respond. Cindy called once more, hoping the cat's curiosity would bring him to the top of the steps. When Cindy reached the top, she was disappointed, but not surprised, to find the cat was nowhere to be seen. Hopefully, he was nearby and she could coax him close enough to scoop him up. She didn't want to have to go all the way back downstairs and grab a package of treats to get the job done.

Cindy flicked the light switch to the left of her head. Casting an eerie yellow glow, the flickering bulb attempted to dispel the darkness, but its feeble light only managed to create distorted shadows on the plywood flooring of the attic. Cindy shivered. Whether or not it was from the cold was up for debate. She looked around quickly, no longer feeling quite so brave.

No cat. Time to skedaddle.

She reached up to flick the switch down when a glint of light flashed across the corner of her eye, commanding her attention. She looked and between two old, wooden chests her eyes fell upon something. A black shoe with a golden buckle. She must have been standing at the right angle for the attic light to reflect off of it when she'd made to turn the light off.

What is that? I've never seen that up here.

Cindy's curiosity was piqued, her unease momentarily forgotten. She walked deeper into the attic and made her way to the shoe.

Her eyes widened in her head. Two large orbs ready to pop out.

It wasn't *just* a shoe, it was a Christmas elf!

She lifted it, slowly at first. The elf certainly had seen better days. It wore a traditional green tunic, the exact sort you'd see an elf wearing on any holiday television special. This one's clothing was very dirty. Cindy caught a faint whiff of mildew. It would need to be washed for sure. The doll had a headful of shaggy, dirty blond, straw-like hair. *He's got more hair than Dad.* She didn't know why the thought crossed her mind but it made her giggle.

The elf's physical condition wasn't much better than the filthy clothes it wore. It was made of some sort of heavy plastic, or so Cindy thought. But there were cracks running along a few parts of the doll's face. Whatever the material was used in its construction, it had a surprising weight to it and felt solid, sturdy. The doll was a stone grey color, an odd choice for sure. Cindy pulled the eyelids up—the hinges still worked —and the doll's eyes were the same dull grey. No pupils, flat solid color only.

The elf's eyes gave Cindy the creeps, so she let them drop closed.

Despite the poor condition of the elf, something about it spoke to her. She'd have to ask Katy, but she thought it might have belonged to her mother, which helped to push aside any feelings of unease.

Cindy was a bit young to believe in concepts like fate, instead, her love for the holiday season led her to believe discovering the elf had been a Christmas miracle. As if everything from the noises upstairs to the wind pushing the attic door open was meant to happen. Cuddling her newly discovered prized possession, she exited the attic and made her way to the basement with a rejuvenated pep in her step. All of her fears and negative thoughts had dissipated as if blown away by the howling wind outside and replaced with seasonal cheer.

It was time to watch the classics!

CHAPTER TWO

Katy honked the horn on her Hyundai Palisade. It had been her mother's vehicle, and after she passed away Katy had begged her father to keep it, save it for her as a sixteenth birthday gift. It took plenty of cajoling; when Jack Feltcher set his mind to something that was usually the end of the conversation, and she knew even looking at the vehicle was painful to her father. Most of Courtney Feltcher's earthly possessions had either been sold, or packed away in a box, collecting dust and rotting. Pretty much what Courtney was doing in her coffin at this very moment.

In the early days after Courtney passed on, Jack and his children fought daily, his eagerness to pack away and forget her existence weighing heavily on his children. Sometimes Katy thought Jack would get rid of the kids to forget about her, if it were an actual possibility. But why should they suffer and lose out on reminders of her simply because Jack couldn't deal with the loss? They were her kids, shouldn't they get a say in the matter?

Katy picked her phone up from the center console and tapped away at the virtual keyboard.

Adam, if you don't get your ass out here now I'm going home and you can walk in the snow.

A text bubble with three dots appeared. Disappeared for a moment before popping up again.

Okay.

"All that just to fucking say *okay*?" Katy knew her brother had probably typed a long wall of smart-ass text and then thought better of it. The chance to get a zinger in hadn't outweighed the potential for him to lose a ride home. Maybe he was smarter than she gave him credit for.

Katy took a hit from her vape pen. She didn't believe for one second these things were as bad as cigarettes. Could they cause harm? Probably. But you weren't going to convince her that the damage done by a vape pen was worse than the cancer sticks people have been sucking down for far longer than she'd been alive. That line of thought was asinine. The difference was the tobacco industry had been around since the 1950s and had more money for lobbyists than the vape industry did.

She waited impatiently for a few more minutes before the light above the porch flickered to life and Adam emerged from the door. She noticed he was already geeking. He had a shit-eating grin plastered across his face, just visible beneath his long, curly hair which had been cut in that corny way teens were styling their hair these days. Katy was only two years older than Adam but she couldn't stand some of the things that had come into style recently. She shook her head as he stumbled to the car, his stupid haircut bobbing up and down with each step.

He opened the door, still smiling and the pungent scent of weed practically slapped her in the face.

"Jesus Christ, Adam. You'd better hope Dad isn't home when we get in. And you'd better throw that shit in the wash and run it. You reek."

"And you reek of failure," he replied.

"That obvious?" she said, cracking a smile.

The zing was a good one, she had to admit. Doubly so because it was true. Ever since Mom had passed she *had* been a failure. Failed to get into college, failed to get a decent job, failed to entice the new pizza cook at Tony's to just go for it when she'd cornered him in the back and made her move.

Her own thoughts spiraled a few hours earlier in the evening when she was alone with the cook and failed to entice him. What the hell was it with guys? It seemed they were either far too grabby, or they needed a written letter of consent. There was no in between.

The owner of the shop had left early for the night, expecting a slow evening due to the weather. At first she was going to close down the restaurant, but decided against it and opted to allow her employees to handle everything.

And boy, had Katy *tried* to handle everything. They'd only been alone for a few minutes before Katy cornered Jimmy, the cook. Continuing her aggressive courting, she'd reached in for a kiss and he'd reciprocated. After a few minutes of making out, she'd grabbed his hands—which until that point had been plastered to his sides—and moved them around her back to cup her ass. He'd left his hands in place, but instead of pulling her in close, he'd jutted his ass out like eighth graders at a dance. Some men couldn't read a hint without a decoder sheet, she knew, so she'd given him an over-the-pants hand job. The moment she'd started rubbing his cock, Jimmy broke the kiss and pushed her away. She'd been so embarrassed she simply went back to her station at the cash register without saying another word.

"Who was the unlucky bastard?" Adam asked.

"The new pizza cook, Jimmy Roberts."

"Wow, that's a new low, even for you."

"Watch it, Adam. Keep talking shit and I'll fuck around with one of your friends and make sure everyone at school knows. Then you'll have to deal with that smoke until you graduate. Nobody will ever let you forget it."

She wouldn't really sleep with one of his friends, she wasn't a pedo. But the look on Adam's face when the words left her mouth told her he believed she'd do it, and that was good enough for her. At least now he'd shut the fuck up and let her wallow in her failure without further commentary.

"Now that you've got that out of your system, we should get home. If Dad gets home before we do, he's gonna be pissed you left Cindy home by herself for so long."

"You're right, but that would require him to be home, and he's never home. He told me this morning he was next up to get forced over to the next shift and he expected it to happen either tonight or tomorrow."

She sighed. "Of course."

Katy pressed the **<DRIVE>** button on the Palisade's gear selection system and they drove home without saying another word.

CHAPTER 3

CHAPTER 3

C had Reynolds sat in the driver's seat of his beat-to-shit green Honda Civic. In his left hand, he held a half-smoked Marlboro between his two fingers, the tip hanging out the window. With his right hand, he aimlessly scrolled through the local news on the cheap smartphone he'd gotten from one of those no contract carriers that sold their plans for dirt cheap. You couldn't get a good phone for free like you could from one of the bigger name brand carriers, but when you'd spent the last fifteen years locked up, even a shitty smartphone was a sight to behold. The leaps and bounds technology had taken were incredible. There was a wealth of knowledge at his fingertips. Long gone were the days of playing *Snake* on a large hunk of plastic with a pixelated screen. He wondered how the math teachers who liked to tell everyone they wouldn't have a calculator with them at all times felt now.

Chad tossed the phone on the passenger seat. He needed to pay attention, not get lost in the wonders of technology. It was bad enough the wind outside whipped up the recently fallen snow and made it difficult to see more than a few feet ahead of you. Any further distractions might cause him to miss his target, setting him back another day.

Chad had been waiting years to get back at Officer Feltcher.

Five years, to be exact.

Chad's early release from prison had been hindered by that super cop son of a bitch, Feltcher. Once Chad had hit ten years served, his sentence became parolable. Lucky for him, ever since the pandemic, the state had been handing out parole like Halloween candy, so long as you kept your nose clean. And Chad *had* kept his nose relatively clean. In comparison to some of his peers, anyway. Well, not really. It wasn't so much that he'd kept his nose clean, rather, he hadn't gotten caught doing anything that would have landed him in hot water. But if you didn't get caught, it didn't happen. On the few occasions he had been caught with contraband or done something stupid, he'd talked the officer out of filing an official discipline report.

Until Feltcher had caught him giving hand jobs in the library for commissary orders.

It wasn't a big deal, really. When men spent that much time behind bars, the lines of sexuality became blurred and guys just wanted to get a nut. They didn't care who the hand was attached to as long as the calluses on it weren't so rough they chafed the shaft. Chad had seen an opportunity and pounced on it. Even now, when he thought about it, he was an entrepreneur. A businessman. But the prison rules didn't see it that way. Any sexual contact was considered rape. Consent didn't exist behind bars. Chad had no money coming into his account, which meant no commissary. Rather than starve, he found a lane and ran it.

After a few weeks, word got out about the man in the back of the library with the soft hands, and Chad's services were now in high demand. So much so that he could bribe the officer who was usually working in the library to look the other way.

It was an easy enough business to maintain. Monday through Friday, when Officer Riggs was at work, Chad would post up between the shelves in the back, giving tug jobs. If the price was right, he'd even swallow the proverbial tube steak.

After months of smooth operation, Chad had become complacent, so when Riggs was on vacation, Chad hadn't even noticed Feltcher sitting at the desk in the corner of the room. He'd been too lost in his own mind, stuck in the Groundhog Day that was life in prison. He'd never heard the jingle of the officer's keys until it was too late. Feltcher busted him churning the butter.

Feltcher was a grade A asshole. There was no paying him off, no bribing him. Not only did that prick bust Chad for a Prison Rape Elimination Act violation, but he'd written a formal discipline report on the bribe attempt too. The very next day, the parole board sent him a letter revoking his parole status. To make matters worse, the letter had told him that because of the severity of violations, he would not be considered for parole at a later time and must complete the last five years of his sentence behind bars.

Out on the streets now, Chad Reynolds was a man with nothing to lose. He had no skills to fall back on, no family to help him out of this bind. And he was homeless, to top it off. If he wasn't sleeping in his car—which he'd gotten from a mutual friend of an inmate he'd worked with inside the prison—he wouldn't have a roof over his head at all. As far as Chad was concerned, it wasn't a matter of *if* he'd end up back in prison, but *when* he'd end up back in prison. For men like Chad, recidivism was an inevitability. What better way to make his grand reentrance into the system than to get payback on that rat fuck, Feltcher.

Through the snow flurries, Chad saw headlights in the

parking lot ahead. He looked at the clock on his phone. It was about time for the prison's shift change. With some luck, this could be Feltcher. Chad already knew the exact vehicle Feltcher drove. When he'd been locked up, his cell had been one with a view of the parking lot from the lone window against the back wall. He watched the lot every morning, learning everything he could about each and every vehicle coming into the lot, even before he'd decided that Feltcher was going to die. Even if he hadn't been able to determine which car was Feltcher's that way, there were a lot of things you could learn about the staff simply from keeping your mouth shut and your ears open. Most of the staff were proud of the vehicles they owned, and the parking lot looked like a luxury dealer's lot. They all liked to talk about what they were driving and the nice things they bought with the large checks they earned working absurd amounts of overtime. So when Feltcher pulled out of the lot in a red and black 2024 Hyundai Kona N Line, there was no question which piece of shit was behind the steering wheel.

Chad let Feltcher get a little way down the road before he pulled out and followed.

He wasn't gonna get the son of a bitch tonight. Tonight would be purely recon. Find out where he lives, get a reading on the neighborhood.

Soon, though, Feltcher would pay dearly.

CHAPTER FOUR

Katy pulled into the empty driveway. Dad still hadn't come home from work, but he hadn't called or texted to let them know he was being held over, so it was possible he would still be home later on in the evening or the early hours of the morning.

Katy knew he liked to stop at the bar for a few drinks after work. It wasn't something he'd ever told her, but Katy was old enough to know a drunk man when he stumbled in the front door. Besides, she'd seen his car at the local dive bar a few times while driving around with friends, so even if he'd tried to deny it, she'd know he was simply trying to save face.

Not that she cared. It wasn't their business if he wanted to have a few drinks on his way home from work. But for some reason, on those nights he would pretend as if there was some sort of emergency at work that required him to stay for a few additional hours but not an entire extra shift.

"Dad's gonna be pissed you didn't take care of the driveway today," she said.

"I'll tell him the blower ran out of gas."

"He's not stupid, you know, just absent. The first thing he's gonna do is check to see if you're lying."

"I'll drain the tank."

"Do you even know how to do that, you moron?"

Adam pursed his lips.

"Didn't think so. Maybe you should just do it now before he gets home."

"As much as I'd love to, Katy, I'm high out of my mind right now and the last thing I'm gonna do is start the snow blower up in the middle of the night. Besides, Ms. Kettle would tell him I was bothering her with it."

Katy laughed. Ms. Kettle was their only neighbor for a good while. The only other house they could see from the driveway. Her house was across the street but probably not close enough for a snowblower to bother her. But that wasn't why Katy laughed. She laughed because it was highly unlikely Ms. Kettle would care, even if she heard. It was a safe bet Ms. Kettle was getting railed at the moment, and if she wasn't, then it was likely one of her many boyfriends would be over shortly to do just that.

Their neighbor was a nice enough young woman, but she had a new guy at her house two or three times a week. Not that Katy thought there was anything wrong with that. Sex positivity was much more acceptable among women now, and slut shaming, while still a thing that occurred, was something that people looked down upon now.

Truth be told, Katy was a little jealous of Ms. Kettle's success with the opposite sex. While the neighbor seemed to have a revolving door of men at her disposal, Katy couldn't find one to save her life. Her friend, Mary, had once told her that she intimidated men. Katy thought it was bullshit, but maybe Mary had been on to something. She was far too pretty to have the level of difficulty she was experiencing with men. There was no real reason she should find it so tough to find a friend with benefits or a one-night stand. Hell, she'd even take a casual relationship, even though she had no interest in being serious with someone.

"What's so funny?" Adam asked.

"Nothing. I think you're fine. Ms. Kettle doesn't give a shit about us. She's never once gotten us in trouble with Dad. Just admit you don't want to take care of the driveway."

"Okay, I don't want to do the driveway."

"Was that so hard? Now get your smelly ass out of my car and get those damn clothes in the washing machine."

The Feltcher siblings exited the vehicle and walked to the front door. Katy punched the code on the keypad and the dead bolt slid open.

She opened the door, calling for her sister as she did so, "Cindy, I'm home!"

"Man, it smells good in here," Adam said.

"Smells like she made gingerbread cookies for Dad again."

"Yeah, too bad he's not here to eat them. As usual. You know, I really don't know why she tries so hard to do shit like that for him. He's never around. She's smart enough to realize that by now."

Katy nodded her head. "She is, you're right. But she's doing it for herself, not for him."

"What do you mean?"

"You really are clueless, aren't you? She loves the Christmas season. She got that from Mom. I think she's just trying to carry on as if Mom were still here and everything is normal."

"Why would she do that? Nothing is normal anymore."

"Because she's twelve, jackass."

They both took their boots off and placed them on the mat next to the door. Adam followed his nose in search of a snack to ward off the munchies. Katy followed. She wasn't hungry —Jimmy had made her a small cheese pizza prior to their incident, which she'd scarfed down in a few brief minutes— but she might grab a cookie or two. If Cindy inherited one skill from their mother before she'd passed, it had been the ability to bake mouthwatering sweets.

As Katy made her way to the dining room a few steps behind Adam, she heard footsteps running up the basement stairs.

"Someone's happy we're home," Katy said.

Cindy burst through the basement door and turned the corner into the dining room so quickly she ran straight into Adam, the impact knocking her on her ass. Adam dropped his cookie, the baked treat breaking into pieces when it hit the floor.

"Watch where—" he said, but stopped short of finishing his sentence.

"Where did you get that?" Katy asked, pointing at the large elf doll Cindy cradled in her arms like a protective mother.

"I found it in the attic."

"What were you doing in the attic? You hate it up there," Adam said.

Cindy blushed. "I started getting a little anxious because nobody was around. The wind was really loud, and I freaked myself out. I was about to go downstairs and watch movies, but I heard something upstairs, like a bump or something. I knew nobody was home because of the cameras and the alarm, so I knew it couldn't be anything bad, probably just Jonesy. But when I looked upstairs I couldn't find him. I was about to go back downstairs when I heard something fall over in the attic. When I got up there, I saw this guy just lying on the ground between some old boxes."

"It's hideous," Adam said.

"It was Mom's," Katy added.

Cindy's eyes lit up. "Really? I thought it might have been hers!"

"I don't remember ever seeing that thing," Adam said.

Katy grabbed the elf from Cindy's arms. "That's because this fine specimen has been missing since we moved from the old house. I hardly remember it myself. What I remember *most* about it was that you were petrified of it, Adam. Dad would always tell Mom to get rid of it, but she refused. You remember how she was with anything Christmas? When we packed everything up for the move, he must have hidden it good because I *vividly* remember her searching for this old thing on multiple occasions. She never found it, though."

Katy looked back at Cindy. "You said this was just in between two boxes in the attic?"

Cindy nodded her head.

"That doesn't make any sense. Mom couldn't have possibly missed it. Even if it wasn't right out in the open, she tore this place apart looking for it."

"I wasn't even looking for it. I was about to shut the attic light off when I caught a reflection or something from the corner of my eye," Cindy said.

Katy threw the elf over her shoulder. "Well, now that that's settled, we can put this raggedy ass doll back in the attic where it belongs."

She made her way back to the front of the house, shifting the elf on her shoulder. It was surprisingly heavy and uncomfortable to carry. How was Cindy running up the stairs with the thing? *That girl is stronger than she looks. Or I'm a hell of a lot weaker than I thought.*

She marched up the steps, Cindy screaming from the dining room to let her keep it. She wanted something special to remember her mother by.

"Sorry, kiddo, but Dad is gonna blow a gasket if he sees this thing. You know how he is with Mom's stuff," Katy said.

She reached the top step when a sharp, burning sensation shot across the back of her neck. She dropped the elf, and it tumbled down the stairs, the heavy plastic hands and head smashing each step on the way down. Each impact sent heavy thumps reverberating through the narrow stairwell. When it reached the bottom, it rolled about a foot before smashing into the front door, ending its journey with a *thwack*.

"Katy, you bitch!" Cindy shouted as she ran to retrieve her mother's elf.

Katy was too busy rubbing her neck to realize what Cindy had called her. She brought her hand to her face, shocked at the blood streaked across her palm and fingertips. What the hell happened? Something had scratched her, but what?

"What the fuck?"

Adam squeezed between the bottom step and Cindy, who had picked up the fallen elf and was clutching it once more. "What's the matter with you?" he asked, a hint of sarcasm in his voice.

"I don't know. I felt something scratch my neck and now I'm bleeding. I don't know if there was a spider from the attic on that thing or maybe a pin or something stuck in its clothing."

Adam pursed his lips and made a face at Katy. "I don't think you'd bleed from a spider bite like that."

"Then there was a splinter or something. It must have been stuck in the shirt and pricked me in the neck when I was adjusting it on my shoulder." The words left her mouth and even she didn't believe them. The splinter theory was a bit more plausible than the spider, but not by much. Would a splinter really draw that much blood? She doubted it. But it was the only explanation she could think of that made any sense.

Adam turned to Cindy. "You'd better not ever talk like that again. Otherwise, I'm going to toss that thing in the fireplace, you hear me?"

Cindy nodded her head. "Does that mean I can keep it?"

"Yeah, Adam said. Just don't let Dad catch you with it. And keep it away from Katy too. I know she said that Dad would flip his lid, but I think it made her sad to see it again. You know how she's been since Mom passed. Why don't you run upstairs and get into bed? I'm going to check out Katy's neck and then I'll be up to read you a story."

Katy heard the comment but ignored it. She noticed, though, that while he was talking to Cindy, he couldn't take his eyes off the elf. Those odd, wacky eyes. Something about them wasn't right. She wasn't surprised he was staring.

"Okay, goodnight, guys," Cindy said, snapping both Adam and Katy out of the trance they seemed to have fallen into. "I made cookies, gingerbread for Dad and chocolate chip for us. There's still a bunch left."

With that, she skipped up the steps cradling her new best friend.

Katy watched her go, and as Cindy slipped past her and turned the corner upstairs, disappearing into her bedroom, she looked at Adam and said, "I don't like that creepy thing."

"Neither do I."

CHAPTER FIVE

Jack Feltcher slowed to a rolling stop in his driveway behind his daughter's vehicle. He gripped the steering wheel until his knuckles turned white. Every night, he pulled up behind Katy's car. Every night, the sight of it made him want to swallow a bullet. Jack's struggle to find the will to live intensified each day. If it weren't for the children, he'd have already killed himself. When his mind was at its worst, it was especially dangerous to be trapped inside of. On those days, he still considered it. During those times when he let his mind spiral, it became difficult to convince himself the kids *weren't* better off without him.

Since Courtney passed, Jack was a shell of his former self. A dried out husk of a human being. He knew that his long hours were fucking up his children and that with the passing of their mother, they needed him more than ever. At first, he told himself he was doing it because it was necessary to keep the bills paid, food on the table, and provide his children with the life he didn't have growing up. But in the depths of his mind—the part that he forced away and only allowed himself to confront when he'd reached the bottom of a bottle—Jack Feltcher knew that, yes, he needed to pick up extra hours to make things work in the current economy as the sole earner, but he didn't need to work nearly as much as he did each week. Eighty-hour weeks used to be something he'd do to put some extra scratch in the bank account, allowing them to build up a nest egg. Or to pay for a Disney trip, or save up for a down payment on a large purchase. But it became an escape after his wife's passing. An unhealthy addiction that was slowly killing him and eroding the mental well-being of his children. Even during the times he allowed himself to acknowledge the negative effect his cowardice had on himself and his children, he felt powerless to change his behavior.

He was an addict. Not to chemical dependency but to running away from the thing that hurt him most: Courtney's memory.

Jack finally let go of the steering wheel and wiped his eyes. Tears streamed slowly down his cheeks and he pawed them away. He looked in the rearview mirror, bleary-eyed. The kids should be asleep by now, but he knew the truth: without an adult to guide them it was unlikely anyone but Cindy was actually asleep. Though they had probably hopped into bed when he pulled into the driveway. As if he didn't know what went on in the house.

A few minutes. That's all Jack needed to clear the pain away.

To make sure the kids wouldn't see him broken down if they were awake when he walked in the door.

Lost in his thoughts, Jack never heard the snow crunching beneath the tires of the beat-up Honda Civic as it crept slowly past him, its headlights turned off.

A vehicle like that stood out conspicuously in this part of town and would have drawn his attention immediately.

Instead, he focused on keeping his shit together for the kids.

CHAPTER SIX

J ack finally made his way inside the house, relieved to find the kids were fast asleep. He kicked his boots off by the door and made his way to the bathroom to take a shower. He turned the water temperature as high as he could bear, relishing the sensation of the scalding water melting away his pain. Or so that was the hope, though it never worked. The hot water running down his body felt good once he'd acclimated to it, and it caused his cock to stir between his legs.

Jack hadn't been with a woman since his wife. He couldn't even bring himself to talk to a woman, let alone take her to bed. He lathered his semihard cock and stroked it, rubbing the head, coaxing it awake. It took a few minutes of working his penis, but eventually he found himself able to achieve a full erection. These days it was taking longer to get hard, even when he was beating his cock hard enough to catch a domestic charge.

Stiff as a board, Jack stroked away but couldn't complete the task. His body was simply too exhausted for creature comforts, such as orgasms. The long hours at work had taken a toll on him, physically and mentally, and his struggles to achieve an erection or reach orgasm were only two side effects of the rigors of his everyday life.

He dreaded going for his upcoming physical exam. It would be his first since his wife's passing and he was sure as shit not the poster child for perfect health.

Jack turned the water off and grabbed the towel, drying off in the shower before stepping out and putting his lounge pants on. He poked his head into both Adam's and Katy's bedrooms but didn't enter. Now that they were older teens, he felt uncomfortable entering their rooms without knocking, especially at night. You never knew what teens were up to. He'd been caught sticky-handed on more than one occasion at their age and swore to himself he'd never embarrass his own children that way.

He approached Cindy's room and gently pushed the bedroom door open. His youngest child and the one most like her mother. Like her siblings, she was growing up too fast. But she was still his baby and somehow he felt far worse letting her down than his two oldest kids. All parents knew it was wrong to have a favorite child, but that didn't mean they didn't have one. Creeping across the hardwood floor, he winced at each creak of the planks. He had no desire to wake her, only to tuck her in. It was chilly. The draft from the attic plummeted the temperature in the room and her covers had come off while she slept.

He grabbed the top of the comforter and pulled it up to her chin. She stirred, eyes fluttering. "Sprinkles," she said.

"Sprinkles?" Jack wasn't sure, but it sounded like she was dreaming about cupcakes or ice cream. "I could really go for chocolate ice cream with sprinkles right now. Thanks, kiddo." He leaned forward and kissed her forehead.

Behind him, something shuffled out of the bedroom door.

That damn cat is always up to no good.

Jack smiled down at his daughter and went downstairs to watch television.

In the corner of the pitch-black bedroom, the closet door slowly opened with an eerie creak that cut through the otherwise silent room. The bones of the house were old, despite the modern updates. Frozen in the doorway, it shook its head, silently cursing the house. "Naughty, naughty," the thing said in a surprisingly deep voice as it slowly exited the closet. "Santa will punish Sprinkles if Sprinkles doesn't do a good job. We can't have that. No, not that."

The elf tiptoed forward a few steps at a time, stopping every so often, pausing as if he was playing some sort of game. Red light, green light, maybe.

It continued forward, humming a tune, occasionally singing the words, "Deck the halls with blood and excrement, fa la la la la . . ." letting the song die on its tongue as it reached the bed.

Sprinkles opened his mouth, a long reptilian tongue breaching the plastic lips of its doll face. He stared at Katy's exposed leg sticking out from under the covers, wishing Santa's magic had gifted him with a different vessel. Instead, he was stuck in a family toy.

No matter, Sprinkles can improvise.

Its heavy, plastic hands caressed Katy's calf. He stopped as a moan escaped her lips and she rolled over. A large bulge grew in the toy come to life's tights, a hint of what the thing intended. Mischief wasn't the only thing he wanted to spread this holiday season.

With one hand, Sprinkles stroked the front of its pants, teasing its member. The other hand hovered just under Katy's slip. Sprinkles gently grabbed her thigh and moved farther up the young woman's leg. He unbuckled the oversized golden belt buckle containing his candy cane and released the plastic cock. It seemed Santa's magic allowed him more freedom than he'd expected. He could work with this vessel. Stroking furiously, he beat his meat like it owed him money until he reached climax. Shuddering, he let out a squeak as jets of red and white seminal fluid erupted from his penis. The melted candy cane-colored baby batter splattered against the side of Katy's mattress, the subsequent weaker spurts of ejaculate landing on her slippers and the floor beneath her bed.

"Oh no," Sprinkles said, giggling. "Naughty elf, who's gonna clean that up?" Sprinkles held his fingers up to his face and licked the candy cane jizz droplets clean. "Mmmm, peppermint."

Sprinkles pulled his tights back up and dashed out of Katy's bedroom, making his merry way down the hall where Adam slept peacefully.

Katy opened her eyes, vision blurry with sleep. She thought she smelled peppermint candy. *Was dad burning candles? What time is it?*

She reached for her phone on the nightstand. Two a.m.

She groaned. It was way too early to be awake, but Jonesy had woken her up. She felt him nuzzling her leg while she slept. She didn't see him in the room. Maybe she'd rolled over in her sleep, scaring him off.

Serves him right for sneaking onto my bed, she thought as her mind faded again, the warm, comforting grip of sleep embracing her once more.

Adam snored. The weed had put him in a deep, dreamless sleep. He'd gotten high out of his mind, doing a "dab"—

smoking the vapors of a super concentrated wax form of cannabis. Bobby, his best friend, had a brother in college who bought the wax for him all the time. Adam hadn't wanted to do it at first. A bong was just fine as far as he was concerned, but Bobby was persistent and wouldn't take no for an answer.

Eventually, Adam had given in. One hit of the concentrate had been enough to send him over the moon.

Sprinkles giggled, interrupting the catchy holiday tune he'd been humming. His eyes sparkled with joy at the prospect of the mischief to come . . . and the mayhem soon after. No doubt that had been the reason Santa chose Sprinkles. Among all of Santa's new breed of mutant elves who'd perished, it was Sprinkles whose essence had been resurrected and poured into the husk it now lived in. Fashioned in the image of Santa's previous helpers, it made Sprinkles sick to his stomach.

It was Sprinkles' hope an exceptional performance this Christmas would earn him his flesh once more.

Sprinkles looked around the room. The possibilities were endless. His large grey eyes fell upon a nutcracker atop a dresser in the bedroom's corner. What better way to please his master than incorporating seasonal imagery into his shenanigans? And when his job was done, tales of what happened would spread. Christmas would never be the same for the Feltcher family.

His candy cane stirred once more.

He climbed the dresser, using each drawer as a step, and snatched the nutcracker, turning and leaping onto the floor. He landed with a thud and stopped in place, ready to run off if the child woke. It was too early to reveal himself.

Sound asleep, Adam had the sort of raging stiffy that only the male teenage body could produce. Careful not to wake his prey, Sprinkles gently opened the flap in the center of Adam's boxers, easing his shaft through the hole. It was more difficult than he expected—while Adam had a rock-hard erection, the boy was cursed with a micropenis, making threading that little needle through anything a chore.

Sprinkles was persistent, though, and got the tallywacker precisely where he wanted it. He lined the nutcracker up and giggled, unable to control himself. Hand over his mouth, he choked back the laughter. Once he was sure that he was done, he grabbed the lever and clamped the nutcracker's mouth down.

Adam shot up from the bed like Linda Blair. He screamed a high-pitched, bloodcurdling scream. No doubt the horrific sound had stirred everyone in the house.

Sprinkles didn't stick around for the welcoming committee to show up. The moment the nutcracker earned its name, Sprinkles took off running like a bat out of hell, his little feet pitter-pattering down the hallway.

While the Feltcher family fought off sleep to tend to Adam, Sprinkles hid, biding his time. There was plenty of time before Christmas.

Plenty of time for fun.

CHAPTER SEVEN

The Feltcher kids were scattered across the basement, the sound of Katy crunching popcorn almost as loud as the television acting as background noise while they ignored whatever was playing in favor of their phones. Cindy sat on the couch, legs crisscrossed with a throw blanket wrapped around her like a cape.

Katy laid back on the recliner, a gigantic bowl in her lap and her phone glued to her hand, mindlessly swiping through TikTok, rarely stopping long enough to watch an entire video. On the love seat, legs spread open, Adam sat with a large ice bag held against his groin.

"Want some popcorn?" Katy asked her siblings.

"No, thank you," Cindy said.

Adam looked at Katy. "Why are you offering, you on a diet or something? That's not gonna help you get laid. The problem is your personality. You can't even get a guy to forget about what a shitty person you are for two minutes."

"That's hilarious coming from the guy who crushed his own penis masturbating with a nutcracker."

Adam's face turned red with shame and he sat up, the sudden movement causing a sharp pain in his groin where the nutcracker had chomped down. He winced and a sharp breath escaped his lips. He paused for a minute, waiting for the pain to subside before speaking, "I told you I wasn't masturbating. I was asleep. One of you assholes did it and you don't want to admit it because Dad will kill you."

"I didn't do anything to you," said Cindy.

"Adam, nobody here cares enough about pranking you to subject themselves to looking at that little baby dick of yours," Katy said.

"Eww, gross!" Cindy exclaimed.

Adam laughed. "Good one, Katy, and maybe that's true, but more than a few of your friends seemed to like it just fine."

Katy threw a handful of popcorn at her brother. Adam had fooled around with more than one of her friends in the last year, a subject that he brought up at any given opportunity. It was why when she would tease Adam that she'd sleep with one of his friends and ruin his remaining years in high school, she was only partially joking. Sometimes, if she were being honest with herself, she thought she'd probably do it.

She wanted to get back at him. Get a little sibling revenge. Two things stopped her from going ahead with it. The first was the fact that all of his friends were sixteen. Katy was no pedo, and while she knew that a sixteen-year-old boy would be more than happy to do the job, she couldn't stoop to that, even if the legal age of consent in Rhode Island was sixteen. Just thinking about it made her feel gross.

The second thing stopping her was that while, yes, Adam had slept with one of her friends and fooled around with at least two more that she knew of, he hadn't made her school life hell by telling anyone about it. Katy didn't think he'd even told any of his own friends, a monumental feat for someone his age. She knew the moment boys his age got any sort of action, their immediate impulse was to shout it from the rooftops. She could only assume Adam had not done so out of respect for her. Even though they often busted each other's chops about anything and everything, at the end of the day they were still close. Since Mom died, they'd all been guilty of getting distant every so often, but the sibling bond had also intensified despite the space they gave each other.

"Seriously, though, I didn't do that. This isn't a teenage raunchy comedy. I don't just stick it in anything with an opening," Adam said.

"Tell that to the nutcracker." Katy winked.

Cindy chimed in. "Not that I want to talk about this with either of you, because gross, but seriously, Adam, if *you* didn't do it, and *we* didn't do it, what do you want us to believe?" she asked, wrinkling her nose in disgust.

"I don't know what to say. The only other possibility that crossed my mind would be that I was so stoned I somehow sleepwalked/sleep-masturbated with the nutcracker? I don't know. That sounds way more insane to me than one of you guys fucking around with me. Although I *was* higher than I've ever been . . ." Adam trailed off. He clearly didn't want to go down that route.

Katy also thought it was absurdly farfetched, but the shit he'd smoked with his buddy had sent him into orbit. Did he throat blast a nutcracker? She didn't know. Was it *possible* he'd done it in some sort of blackout state? She thought so, even if she didn't believe it to be the truth.

"Dad said you still have to take me sledding tomorrow," Cindy said, changing the subject.

"Yep, I know. Katy, you're gonna have to drop us off, though. I can manage being there. My junk seems to be on the mend but I'm still sore. I definitely can't walk there and back," Adam said.

Katy sighed. The responsibility of playing the role of second parent was exhausting. She loved her brother and sister, but she wasn't their mother. Why should she be forced to pick up the slack because Dad was burying himself in work?

Just as Katy opened her mouth to complain, Adam spoke again, "I get it, Katy. But not right now. I'm not in the mood for it, and you know Dad is gonna make you anyway, so why bother arguing? We're only going to the slopes near the lottery building. It's on your way to work, so it's not that big of a deal. I'll make sure Cindy is ready to go by the time you're leaving for work, so you don't need to worry about being late."

Katy was shocked, her brother's response unexpected. He was usually the last person to ask for a break in the ball busting and arguing. It must be the holiday season. Sometimes Katy forgot that her brother didn't erect the same defensive walls she did, and the loss of their mother would naturally feel stronger this time of the year.

"Okay," she said, "but I'm not waiting, so make sure you're ready or I'm leaving without you."

"Thanks, Katy! You're the best!" Cindy said.

Adam smiled, the heaviness already evaporated from his mood. "So what are we gonna do for Christmas Eve? Dad already said he had to work."

"I don't know, I was gonna have a friend over," Katy said.

"Yeah, I guess I'll see if Bobby wants to come chill. His family isn't big on Christmas, so I'm sure they won't mind as long as he's back early."

Cindy chimed in. "I've got my friend right here!" she said, cradling the elf.

"You call that hideous thing a friend?" Adam asked.

"Hey! This was Mom's. Don't be a jerk!"

"'Don't be a jerk!'" Adam repeated in a mocking tone. "Why don't you put the damn thing down? Or throw it in the fireplace where it belongs? No wonder Dad hid that piece of shit in the attic."

Katy laughed. "You're right, that thing *is* disgusting. But she has a point. For some reason, Mom loved it. If she wants to carry it around like a baby blanket, I say let her."

"You guys are no fun," Adam said as he snatched a pillow from beside him and cocked his arm back. He launched the pillow, and with pinpoint accuracy, it nailed Sprinkles, sending him flying out of Cindy's grasp.

"Hey!" Cindy shrieked.

"I'm going to bed. Get rid of that thing," Adam said. He eased off the love seat and walked gingerly up the basement steps, favoring his injured groin.

"I wish someone would teach that asshole a lesson," Cindy said.

"Yeah, sometimes I do, too," Katy agreed.

CHAPTER EIGHT

Chad had knocked back a shot of Jose Cuervo and signaled the bartender over. It surprised him to find his old stomping grounds, Billy's Frosted Mug, still around after all the years he spent locked up. The name had changed, but the ownership remained the same. A simple case of rebranding in order to give the business a shot in the arm and remain relevant. Chad couldn't understand why they went through the trouble of rebranding and putting up new signs, but didn't bother to renovate the interior or attract a different customer base. It seemed like a recipe for failure to him, though he was no businessman.

The bartender, Christina, made her way over to Chad and nodded her head in acknowledgment. "Same thing?" she asked.

"Let me take one more Cuervo and a Bud Light, baby doll."

"Jesus, can you get any cornier? You can call me Christina, or you can walk your ass out of the bar."

"Who's gonna make me? I've been coming here since you were in diapers."

"Oh yeah? I've never seen you before tonight, and I've been here for almost five years now."

"They don't exactly give furloughs for bar visits when you're locked up for killing a man, sweetheart. Now why don't you get my drinks?"

If Christina had a response to that, she kept it to herself. She walked away and took her sweet-ass time before returning with his drinks. And Chad's tab.

"Finish your drinks. I'm closing you out. You walk out of here on your own, or I can have the Glenwood Police Department escort you. I'll leave that one up to you."

"That's all I wanted, sweet thang." Chad knocked back the shot and chased it with the entire bottle of beer, finishing it in one chug. He slammed the empty bottle down, threw a fifty-dollar bill on the bar top, and spun the stool 180 degrees, hopping off while it still spun.

He was hungry and drunk. The room took on the hazy quality alcohol brings and he knew he was a few drinks away from the spins, which was right next door to puking. Chad had a few more bills left from the wallet he'd stolen earlier that day and had a mind to walk a few blocks down the street and grab something to eat at The Big Cheese Pizza. They made a delicious pie, and as a bonus, at the rear of the establishment was a small bar. He could wash down his pepperoni and cheese with another Bud Light. That should be enough to put him in the sweet spot. Drunk enough to dull the pain of his existence, but not so drunk he'd be stuck puking his brains out.

An hour later, after demolishing an entire large pizza by himself and getting kicked out of The Big Cheese for slapping his server's ass, Chad found himself puking in the alleyway behind the restaurant. Chunks of cheese and pepperoni splattered the snow, the mixture of Cuervo, Bud, and pizza steaming in a pile a few feet from his face. When the last of the vile stew had erupted from his stomach, Chad stood up, slowly. No need to tempt fate again. Dry heaves were always worse than the puke that had come before.

He wiped the chunks from his lips, smearing the putrid liquid across his beard and mustache.

Snow crunched behind him and a bell rang.

"Ho Ho Ho. It appears someone had a bit too much eggnog tonight," said a voice from behind him.

Chad turned around, his head pounding.

The voice belonged to a guy dressed in a Santa costume. He had a black container in one hand, filled to the brim with cash, and a large golden bell in the other. The man walked past Chad, chuckling to himself.

He kept ringing the bell as he passed, and the sound of it pierced Chad's ears. A pain like someone drilling a hole through his skull.

"Why don't you mind your business?" Chad pinched the bridge of his nose with his thumb and index finger. "And would you stop with that fucking bell? My head is pounding."

"Stop? I can't stop ringing the bell, son. I'm here to spread holiday cheer. Clearly, you could use some!"

Was that imposter Santa seriously mocking him? Chad's world turned red. His head still throbbed from projectile vomiting, but now his temples were pounding, too, a result of his rapidly rising blood pressure. He couldn't believe the nerve of that fucker. *Holiday cheer, huh? I'll give you something that's gonna cheer* me *right the fuck up, you son of a bitch.*

Fists clenched, Chad forgot all about the steaming pile of liquified pizza his body had ejected and watched Santa continue on his merry way. He let the red-suited bastard get some distance and turn down an adjoining alleyway before he acted. Once Chad was sure the man couldn't see him, he grabbed a discarded beer bottle from the snow next to the overflowing dumpster. He smashed the bottle against the brick wall and stalked after jolly ole Saint Nick.

They traveled a few blocks like that, Santa Claus ringing his bell and flaunting his bucket full of cash, Chad tailing him, careful not to reveal himself until the right moment.

Santa stepped out from the alley and into what had once been a large, bustling industrial zone. Now, the area was barren of life, aside from rodents and other pests. He continued walking a few hundred feet and stopped in front of an abandoned factory, the windows and entryways all boarded up. Spray paint tags and graffiti decorated the building and boards. The usual suspects were there: tag names, gang iconography, names and numbers to call for a good blow job.

Santa placed his bell and bucket of cash on the ground before turning his head conspiratorially, apparently checking if the coast was clear, before returning his attention to the blocked doorway. He gripped the large sheet of wood and pulled it aside. It seemed to move with ease, as if placed for show rather than function. Maybe the appearance of a secure building was enough to keep inquisitive wanderers at bay.

With the blockade out of the way, the vagrant Santa picked his belongings up and placed them on the other side of the threshold before crossing it himself and sliding the board back into place.

"What have we got here, Santa? What's behind door number one?" Chad asked himself.

Chad swiftly made his way across the lot, his eyes scanning the area, checking for any spectators. When he was satisfied there was nobody around, he made his move. Sliding the board aside and following the man into the derelict building.

It was dark inside. Floating dust motes clouded the room. Cobwebs decorated the ceiling and corners of the room. With each step, Chad's nostrils caught a hint of smoke amidst the ever-present stench of piss and shit.

He continued forward, following the orange glow and wisps of smoke trailing through the building. In the next room, he discovered the source of the smoke.

Standing in the center of the room, Santa. He had disrobed and stood in front of a large metal drum, wearing only a pair of dirty boxer shorts. A fire blazed within the drum, warming the room and keeping the area lit. Chad could see no other occupants in the room, only the homeless Santa who'd obviously been roleplaying as a Salvation Army Santa to prey upon the goodwill of people during the holiday season.

For some reason, this further enraged the inebriated Chad Reynolds, as if impersonating that organization's Santa was so much worse a crime than those that he himself had committed. And the ones he still intended to commit in the near future. The vagrant had a nice little setup going, and if Chad was honest, it was better than the homeless shelter he'd been staying at.

Chad's vehicle—which had doubled as his home, which he preferred to staying in a shelter—broke down and was recently towed by the town of Glenwood. He had no money to retrieve the vehicle, never mind pay to have it repaired.

The building where Chad found himself grew more appealing by the minute. Once he finished with the bum, he'd take over his territory, stake claim on it as his own. He only needed a place to stay until he'd taken care of Feltcher. After that, he fully expected it wouldn't be long before the police apprehended him and then he'd have a one-way ticket back to his real home, Glenwood Correctional Institute. After fifteen years of acclimation to the prison system, he much preferred it to living on the streets. In prison, he had three meals a day, a job—even if it was only sexual favors for money—and access to television. Hell, he even had a tablet. And that thing never got shut off for nonpayment. He'd already missed the payment on his phone and had the damn thing canceled.

And from what Chad saw of the man's cash bucket, it appeared as if he'd made a decent amount of money ripping off kindhearted passersby. Probably more than enough to hold Chad over until he settled the score with Feltcher.

Everything he needed for the immediate future was right here: cash and a roof over his head.

To the victor belong the spoils of the enemy. Or something like that, Chad thought.

The homeless man picked up the bucket and started counting his haul, unaware he'd soon have no use for it. His iconic red and white garb hung on a clothesline, drying over the fire. Water dripped from it, hitting the floor with a *plink* that echoed through the room.

Chad crept up behind the vagrant, his head suddenly clear, laser focused on his target. If it weren't for the lingering taste of vomit, he could have sworn he hadn't touched a single drop of alcohol.

A few feet from the man, Chad stepped on a piece of broken glass, crunching it underneath his boot. The bum spun around. "Who's that? What are you doing here?"

The kill wouldn't be as clean as Chad hoped. While a stealth attack was no longer possible, he still had a moment to strike while the bum was caught off guard. Chad rushed him, closing the last few feet of distance and raising the broken beer bottle overhead. The man recovered and stepped aside, quicker than Chad would have thought possible—either that or he was not as sober as he thought he was—and dodged the sharp brown bottle. The blow, intended for the man's throat, only nicked the skin of his shoulder.

"Hey man, we can talk about this! I was just busting your chops earlier. It's not that serious," the man said.

"I told you to stop ringing that bell, you piece of shit."

The vagrant backed up a step, both arms in front of him with his palms out as if he could talk Chad out of it. On his chest, open sores wept, oozing a milky white pus. Scabs adorned his arms and face. His large, red nose screamed alcohol abuse.

The man's hideous appearance repulsed Chad, stirring his vomit reflex once more. He needed to be rid of this man. Taking a quick half step forward, Chad feinted, baiting the man. The hobo fell for it, swatting his arm down in defense of a stab that never came. When the man swatted down, Chad swung the bottle in a wide arc over his arm.

This time, his aim had been true.

The bottle found a home on the left side of his cheek, tearing the flesh, piercing the eyeball. A grotesque combination of ocular fluid and blood ran down his cheek, leaving a sticky trail. It looked like a gelatinous mixture of ketchup and mayonnaise.

The man howled in pain, but Chad offered no quarter. He was fueled by a murderous rage; he stabbed and sliced, poked and prodded with the beer bottle. He drove it into the man's body repeatedly, feeling the resistance of flesh give way with each brutal thrust. The bottle broke again, cutting Chad's hand, but he didn't notice the pain. He'd simply tossed the weapon aside and pummeled the homeless man's trembling body.

Blood pooled at Chad's feet. He picked the man up and carried him toward the burning barrel. The man's chest rattled with each breath. He coughed, spraying blood everywhere, but didn't have the energy to resist.

With a grunt, Chad hefted the man up and into the barrel. The flames licked over his body, hungrily devouring every inch of him.

Chad clenched his fists, staring at the man. His mind lacked thoughts, eyes devoid of emotion.

After a few minutes, the nauseating smell of burning flesh

and hair jolted Chad out of his trance. "Merry Christmas, motherfucker," Chad said to himself.

He laughed, picking up the bucket of cash. The spoils of war. Chad pulled a wad from the bucket and counted his bounty.

A breeze from a broken window somewhere down the hall chilled the room, despite the fire. Chad stopped counting the money, stared at the Santa costume fluttering on the line.

The distraction sparked a plan in his mind. A grin crept across his face, exposing rotten, blackened teeth as the flames consumed the vagrant's battered corpse.

CHAPTER NINE

Katy dropped Adam and Cindy off at the sledding hills. Adam had promised their father he would keep a close eye on his younger sister. Although the sledding hills over by the lottery building were used by what seemed like every family that lived in the town of Glenwood, the proximity to the busy main road terrified Jack, and he'd badgered Adam for hours the night before about safety, as if Adam didn't know being hit by a moving vehicle was deadly.

As far as anyone knew, there had never been an instance of a vehicle hitting a child while sledding in the area. The hill was extremely steep, perfect for picking up speed. But once you reached the bottom, it climbed steeply uphill. It was impossible for anyone to reach the peak and make it onto the road.

According to Jack, that wasn't what he was worried about. His biggest fear was of a vehicle losing control and careening off the side of the road, barreling into the children. Cindy wished her father had confided his worries to Adam in private because from the moment she'd heard the words leave his mouth, the image of a car sliding down the embankment and into a row of kids riding tubes and sleds burned itself into her brain. Now, she was too petrified to sled down the hill.

Besides, Jonesy was missing and she couldn't concentrate on having fun when the family cat could be hurt, or lost, or worse—eaten by a coyote. She'd asked Adam if they could just stay home, but Dad had already forced him to cancel his plans for the morning so he could watch her. That had pissed Adam off, so rather than stay home and hang out, he decided if he was to suffer, she would too.

Cindy didn't understand why Adam acted like such a jerk all the time. Katy too. Mom was gone, and at twelve, Cindy understood they were all dealing with it in different ways. But that didn't mean everyone had to behave the way they did. It made no sense to her why she, the youngest in the family, seemed to be the only member *not* falling apart. It wasn't fair. *She* should be the one lashing out. *She* should be the one misbehaving, doing poorly in school. Her brother and sister were old enough that they should be able to deal with it, not her.

Dad at least had a better excuse, in her opinion. He was doing the work of two adults now. Cindy forgave him for not being around as much as she liked. But even though she thought Dad had a better excuse than her siblings, she still thought he was handling things wrong. There had to be some way where he could be around more often, even if it was only a bit more.

And he smelled funny too. She knew he was drinking too much alcohol, but what could she say to him? At twelve, she was old enough to understand things much better than her family gave her credit for, but not old enough that she felt she could voice her opinion on the things going on around her.

Playing children and watchful parents packed the sledding hills to the brim. Had Cindy actually been playing, it might have been difficult for Adam to keep watch with all the action going on. Instead, she sat on a bench in the back of the area at the border of the woods. She clutched her elf and hummed Christmas carols while she waited for Adam to finish up. She was bored out of her mind, but when Adam had walked off with his friend, he had said nothing to her. Who knew how long he'd be gone? He couldn't have gone far. Dad would whoop his ass if he left her alone for long. Still, it would be nice to have an expectation of when he'd return rather than sitting around with no clue what was going on.

Snow crunched ahead of her, but she was staring at the snow beneath her own boots, and didn't notice anyone approach until a pair of black boots appeared seemingly out of nowhere.

Cindy looked up. Carl Anderson, the meanest eighth grade bully, stood before her. Carl was a real piece of shit, and Cindy didn't feel bad thinking about him in that way. He was bad news. In trouble all the time for beating up the other students. His pranks were always mean-spirited, never funny. Like the time he smeared dog shit in Laurie King's locker. Or the time when he forced Timmy Rice to drink piss from a bottle Carl had found behind the school. She'd never forget the look on Timmy's face the moment the yellow liquid touched his lips. Or the way he projectile vomited after the first gulp. That was the last time Timmy had shown up at school. He'd been homeschooled ever since.

Thinking about the awful smell of the pee bottle and Timmy's puke turned her stomach, and it took great effort for her not to lose her lunch right there in the snow. If she puked on Carl's boots, there was no telling what he'd do to her.

Please hurry, Adam, she thought.

"What the fuck are you staring at, Feltcher?" Carl asked.

She snapped out of her trance. She must have spaced out. Had she been staring at him? No, definitely not. "I wasn't staring," she responded.

"Mmmhmmm. Sure you weren't. You want a piece of this?" Carl asked, making a crude gesture at his crotch.

The comment repulsed Cindy. Her face betrayed her thoughts.

"What's that look for, Feltcher? You think you're too good for me? Is that it?"

"No, not at all. I don't think that."

"Good, because you're not. You're not even good enough to keep your mom. I heard she quit fighting. She wanted the cancer to kill her because she couldn't stand having a fuckup like you for a daughter."

Tears welled up behind Cindy's eyes. She fought them back. It wasn't true. Cindy's mom didn't want to die because of her. She knew Carl was being a jerk. But knowing it wasn't true didn't make the comment hurt any less.

Still, she refused to let the bully see her cry.

"What's the matter? That hideous elf got your tongue? God, where did you find that thing? It's uglier than you."

"He's not ugly! He's just old. He was my mom's. You take that back," Cindy yelled at Carl. She'd had enough of his shit. Making fun of Mom, and now one of the few possessions of her mother's she had access to.

"You know what? I'll take it back. I'll take this damn thing back to the dump where it belongs!" Carl said as he snatched the elf from Cindy's grasp. Carl sped off, running into the woods. He'd taken her by surprise, putting plenty of distance between the two of them and was well into the woods before she'd reached the tree line.

She wouldn't let that stop her, though. No way in hell she was going to let some asshole bully take her mom's elf.

Katy leaned over the countertop, her chin resting on her hands, blowing and popping an enormous piece of gum. It was obnoxious, she knew, but there were no customers at the moment and she was bored. Through the windows on the double doors, she peered into the kitchen.

Jimmy stood in front of the oven with his head down. It looked like he was scrolling through his phone, but from where Katy stood, it was difficult to be sure. Once again, the two of them were alone manning the restaurant. It was the first time they'd been alone together since the *incident*. Neither of them had spoken a word to the other since that awkward moment, but Katy was ready to lay the cards on the table once more. Her father always quoted some sports adage, "You miss one hundred percent of the shots you don't take," and it annoyed the hell out of her when he said it, but there was an undeniable truth to it. And in this moment, it was the first thing to flash in her mind, spurring her into action.

"Fuck it," she said, walking toward the kitchen. It was now or never. The rejection had pissed her off, and to be honest, stung a little. What the hell was so wrong with her that it seemed like she couldn't throw herself at a guy? She felt like the only woman on the planet who had this problem. She was going to walk in there and see what the hell his problem was. He wasn't married—far too young for that— had no kids, no girlfriend. It hadn't occurred to Katy that he might not be into women until she shoved the door open. By the time the thought crossed her mind, she was already in the kitchen, spilling her guts.

Jimmy listened, taking in every word that came from her mouth.

Katy couldn't tell what was running through his mind. His face was a blank slate. Was he even listening?

She continued on, not giving him a chance to speak until

he interrupted her mid-sentence. "Katy, stop talking for a minute."

She stopped, shocked at the bluntness.

"I don't know what the hell you're talking about. I didn't blow you off. There's nothing wrong with you. You're not like, hideous, or anything like that."

"So what is it?"

"If you let me continue and don't interrupt, I'll tell you."

"Okay."

He shot her a look. She made a lip zipping gesture.

"I can't speak for everyone, but for me, the problem isn't *a* problem. There are a few. First off, you come on way too strong. Don't get me wrong, that night was like a fantasy for most dudes, I guess, but when it came down to it, it was actually a turnoff. The other thing, which to me is an even bigger deal than you coming on too strong, you're not really a pleasant person to be around since . . ." he trailed off.

"Since my mom died?"

"Yeah, I didn't want to say it, but yeah. Since she passed you're . . . abrasive? I don't know if it's the right word, but you're kind of a bitch."

"My fucking mom died, you dick."

"Yeah, I get it, and obviously that's tough, but the way you act, people don't want to be around you."

Katy sighed. She wasn't buying the part about her coming on too strong, thought it was bullshit. It seemed like a cop-out to her. But he'd also said there was nothing physically wrong with her, and the two complaints he'd mentioned were something that she could see keeping people away, so maybe there was truth to it after all.

"Okay, I get it. I guess that makes sense. I'm not sure I really agree with it, but I can see why that would be a problem. But things have been tough, ya know? My mom died, my dad is never home, and I'm the one stuck taking care of my brother and sister. I shouldn't be the one taking care of them. That's not my job. Your parents are supposed to be the ones who pick up the pieces. The ones to tell you everything is going to be okay, even if it doesn't seem like it. But I'm doing it. I want to have fun again. I want to be an eighteen-year-old. Carefree, happy. How the hell am I supposed to do that when I haven't had the chance to cope with losing her because I had to *replace* her?" She looked down at her feet, embarrassed at how much she'd blurted out to Jimmy. It had been a mistake. She hardly knew him.

Jimmy didn't respond, just stood there with his hands in his pockets. The question must have stumped him, much the same as it had stumped Katy for the last few months. She felt her lip quiver but pushed back the tears that had been building up.

Jimmy slowly leaned forward, as if unsure about what he was doing, before at last embracing Katy, pulling her close. "I don't know how you're supposed to manage all of that. I don't think I could. I'm sorry. I guess I never thought about how tough you had it. I feel bad now."

"For what?"

"You know, for thinking you are a bitch."

They both laughed, and Jimmy let her go.

Katy smiled but didn't know what to do next, so she turned around and started back toward the front of the store, where she could be embarrassed in solitude.

"Hey, wait," Jimmy said.

Katy turned around. "Yeah?"

"What about if we hung out? Take it a little slower. I'm not saying act like we're in middle school, ya know, but maybe we don't go straight for the groin. Maybe save that for the second date."

"I'd like that," she said, laughing. "So how about Christmas Eve? My dad is working that day. He goes in at three p.m. and usually works until eleven, and honestly, he will probably head in early that morning too. But with the storm coming, he might even stay overnight and not come home until seven the following morning. Anything after sixteen hours he gets paid double time, and he usually won't turn down the opportunity for that kind of pay. I really don't think Christmas Day will be any different. If anything he'll justify it by saying he was still home for dinner Christmas Day."

Jimmy looked at her, clearly shocked. She wasn't sure at which part. The long hours? Or that her father would probably choose to work overtime rather than spend the holiday with his children. Likely both of those things. Most people were surprised when they found out how much Jack worked.

"My family doesn't really do anything on Christmas Eve, so I can make that work. The storm is supposed to be a rough one, though. I'm probably gonna have to crash at your place."

Katy shrugged. "I know," she said. "If you're worried I'm gonna come on too strong again, you can sleep in the basement. We had it finished last year. It's nicer than my bedroom." She smiled.

"All right, it's a date," Jimmy said.

Katy flashed another smile and almost moved in to kiss Jimmy before thinking better of it. He'd already told her she moved too fast. She thought she'd take his advice, move slower this time. From what she knew of Jimmy, he seemed a better guy than most men their age. Maybe this was what she needed after all the stress she'd been through lately.

Leaving the kitchen, she felt invigorated with a newfound excitement for the future. Things were looking up after all.

Carl Anderson cradled the elf in his arm, running through the snow-covered woodland like an NFL running back punching through a hole in the defensive line. He was going to make sure that little Goody Two-shoes never saw this hideous piece of trash again. What the hell was she doing carrying it around, anyway? The thing looked like it had been through the Vietnam War and somehow lived to tell the tale. The dingy, green costume was so disgusting with filth that his skin crawled merely from the doll touching his jacket. He'd be sure to take a nice hot shower when he got through with this thing. Maybe he'd burn the jacket just to be safe.

As he ran through the trees, the bells on the elf's slippers jingled with each step Carl took. The thing was oddly heavy, and he had to keep readjusting his grip on it. Still pumping his legs, Carl thought he heard someone laughing. He slowed down, trying to figure out where it had come from. Between the snow crunching underfoot and the swish of his snowsuit, it was hard to hear anything in the winter wonderland.

Hehehe.

There it was again. The sound was creepy and made the hair on the back of his neck stand on edge.

This time, Carl knew where it came from.

The elf.

"Did they really put a voice box in this thing that sounds like a fucking pedo?" Carl asked himself.

He held the doll out in front of him, turning it about. It was difficult to tell because of the elf's tunic, but Carl saw no sign of a voice box. Maybe there was a compartment built into the body. He thought if there was one, it might be funny to rip the thing out and use it to prank people somehow. The voice was that creepy.

Carl took his gloves off. With them on, his fingers would lack the dexterity required to pry open whatever compartment housed the box and batteries that likely powered the elf.

Exposed to the elements, his hands were cold and stiff. He worked the tunic up but could see no opening on the back, only a solid, hard plastic shell. He knocked on the elf's body.

The thing sure was sturdy. He flipped it once more, taking in the unsightly features of Santa's little helper.

"One ugly motherfucker," Carl said.

As if in response to Carl's voice, the elf's eyes shot open, revealing dull, grey orbs that were the same color as its body.

The color of a gravestone.

"Ya gonna feel me up like that and there's not even mistletoe around? What kind of sexual deviant are you?" the elf asked. *Tee-hee-hee.*

"What the fuck? What kind of joke is this? Since when do they make toys that say shit like that?"

"I'm not a toy, you naughty little shit, I'm Sprinkles. Want a candy cane?" Sprinkles flicked his wrist, invoking Santa's Christmas magic. A candy cane materialized. With a sinister grin on his face, Sprinkles clutched the oversized, red and white striped treat in his hand. Pointy, needlelike teeth filled the elf's mouth. Too many teeth, like a shark. Carl didn't think his teeth had looked like that a moment ago.

Carl was stunned. He couldn't believe what was happening. This had to be a dream or a hallucination. He must have hit his head while sledding. But it wasn't a dream, and as soon as he noticed the candy cane Sprinkles waved was not only approaching a foot in length, but it had a wicked tip that appeared to have been whittled down to a point like a holiday-themed prison shank, he dropped Sprinkles to the ground.

Sprinkles swung the candy cane as he fell to the snow. Carl's unexpected drop of the elf had saved his life; the candy cane missed hitting his eyeball by a few inches. It did still find a home, however, slashing across the bully's rosy cheeks, tearing the skin as easily as a chef-filleted fish. A flap of meat hung down, exposing red sinew and gristle. Behind the strands of skin and tissue, the white of Carl's teeth were exposed.

Carl dropped to his knees and screamed, a tortured

mixture of pain and terror. The animalistic howl of primal fear. The predator finally learning what it felt like to be prey.

Sprinkles darted forward and dove at Carl, who was no longer paying attention to the elf but holding his hand over his mangled cheek, screaming hysterically. Blood gushed from the wound, leaking between Carl's fingers and spilling onto the snow beneath him.

Sprinkles' body collided with Carl, and the monstrous elf clamped his shark teeth on the boy's nose, wrenching his body back and forth like a dog with a rope. The cartilage crunched under the force of Sprinkles' bite, blood spurting all over the elf and Carl.

The crimson liquid sloshed into the back of Carl's mouth and down his throat, gagging him with the very liquid that gave him life. Sprinkles bit down harder and placed his white-gloved hands on Carl's shoulders. The elf pushed, using both legs to gather a greater force, tearing Carl's nose from his face, leaving nothing but a hideous, ragged, bleeding orifice.

Sprinkles spat the boy's nose in the snow and stood over his prone body. Brandishing the weaponized candy cane, the elf leaned down and drove the point through Carl's ear, piercing through the soft membrane inside and ripping the vertebral artery.

Carl convulsed on the ground, his body jerking and spasming as blood gushed from his face, nose, and ear.

"I like to get straight to the point," Sprinkles said, giggling as he spoke to the dying boy.

A voice called from the woods, "Carl! Just give it back! My mom gave him to me. Please!"

Sprinkles snapped his fingers, once again invoking Santa's magic. In the blink of an eye, the candy cane disappeared and Sprinkles' gore-covered tunic returned to its former state— faded and dingy, with a hint of mildew, but free and clear of Carl's blood.

The elf took a few steps back. Its eyes snapped shut, and it dropped to the snow, a few feet from where Carl Anderson bled out.

Cindy emerged from the trees, saw the horrific scene, and screamed.

CHAPTER TEN

Jack Feltcher gripped the steering wheel in his hands, white-knuckling the leather steering wheel. The drive home from the police station was excruciatingly slow. Between the weather forcing Jack to keep the speed to a minimum and the cemetery silence in the car, it seemed as if they had been driving for hours.

Adam sat in the passenger seat, leaning back and looking out the passenger window. He hadn't looked his father in the eyes since the moment Jack arrived at the police station. Adam had fucked up royally, something both father and son agreed on.

Jack was a ticking time bomb, ready to explode. Another fact everyone in the car knew. In the back seat, Cindy gripped the elf, tears streaming from her eyes. Jack knew his daughter was petrified, and for good reason.

She could have easily been in the same situation as Carl Anderson. Based on Cindy's statement to the police, the boy had possibly still been alive when she stumbled across his mangled body. Prior to that, she claimed he'd been perfectly fine only a few minutes earlier when the boy had stolen her toy and ran off.

Initially, things hadn't looked good for Cindy, and the police had told Jack as much when he arrived at the station. They found no weapon, no evidence to speak of, and Cindy didn't have a drop of blood on her. But they had motive—the prior bullying—and they had Cindy at the scene of the crime. About an hour and a half later, while investigating officers combed through the woods of the surrounding area, they discovered a man named Peter O'Toole living in a tent close to where Carl was murdered.

Peter O'Toole was a homeless man, five times convicted for possession of child pornography. But a judicial system that was tougher on selling drugs than it was on kiddie fiddlers meant O'Toole was a free man despite his crimes against children. The convictions made it tough for O'Toole to find suitable housing. Unable to find a place to rent or a group home to take him in, Peter had been staying at the local homeless shelter. But with the cold weather arriving, the homeless shelter was crowded, and with the shelter being available on a first-come-first-serve basis, it wasn't a guarantee he'd have a bed each night. He'd have to show up early every day and hope there was a vacant cot. Rather than deal with that, Peter took up residence in the woods.

When the detectives questioned him, he'd claimed that he had nothing to do with Carl's death. Peter told the detective his tent in the woods helped for two reasons. The first, the overcrowded nature of the shelter. The second, the temptation he felt in the proximity of young boys and girls.

Peter O'Toole told the truth about not murdering Carl Anderson, but his reasoning about the children didn't add up. And the detectives weren't buying it. They knew children frequented the area all winter long. To them, it made little sense for him to stay in those woods if the objective was to distance himself from children. Peter had chosen the woods to avoid the shelter, yes, but he'd chosen *that* area of the woods because he *liked* to be near the kids. He hadn't killed

Carl Anderson, but it would have only been a matter of time before he preyed on another child.

From speaking with the detectives, Jack learned they were charging Peter with the boy's murder. There was no solid evidence of his guilt. In fact, the only thing they had on O'Toole was that he was a child predator who happened to be in the area. It was their hope that with a public defender in Peter's corner and a record like his, the jury would be so hell-bent on justice they'd convict him on circumstantial evidence alone.

Jack thought it was more likely than not that O'Toole would go to prison. He couldn't say he cared. Even if the man was innocent of Anderson's murder, he still belonged in prison. The only downside he saw to a wrongful conviction was it meant the real child killer would be on the loose.

"Anything you want to say, Adam?" Jack asked.

Adam shook his head.

"I'm talking to you. I expect a response."

"And I shook my head no. That's a response."

"Listen, you little prick, I don't need the smart-ass comments right now. Why the fuck weren't you watching your sister? That could have been her. If she'd been there a few minutes sooner, it *would* have been her. And then what would you have to say for yourself? That someone took your sister from us because you couldn't wait to get high."

"I wasn't—"

Jack didn't let him finish. "Shut your fucking mouth. I'm not stupid. You might think you're smart. You might think you're getting one over on me. You're not. You get away with it because I choose not to press the issue. I choose to let it slide. I let you think you got one over on me because I remember what it was like to be your age. I know what life is like for a teenager."

"You know what it's like, Dad? Why don't you tell me what it feels like for your mother to die on you before you had time to do anything with your life? Why don't you tell me what it feels like to carry on every day with one dead parent and one parent who is never around?"

"Damn it, Adam. I'm doing my best. I'm trying to be there for you guys. I'm trying to give you the life I never had and I'm doing it alone now. I don't have anyone to help me through this either. All I have is you kids."

"You don't have us, Dad! You're never around. You and I both know it's not *only* about paying the bills and giving us a better life. You're avoiding being home because it reminds you of Mom. You could easily cut down on the overtime, even one or two shifts a week, and we would be fine. It wouldn't financially ruin us. I'm not stupid. We all know how much you make. You brag about it all the time. I don't want a fucking trip to Universal Studios. I don't care about fancy new cars. I want my mom and dad to be there for me. Mom's dead, so she can't do that. You? You might as well be dead, as much as you're not around."

Adam Feltcher's outburst stunned his father to silence. Jack was pissed, but his son's scathing outburst left him tongue-tied. Adam's attack wasn't without merit, but he also felt like it was an exaggeration. Teenage overdramatization. Adam had a right to be upset, Jack knew that, but even if Jack were to admit his son was right, and he was an absent father, it didn't change the fact Cindy had been only a few minutes away from being the victim of a crime rather than the person to discover one.

"Adam, I hear what you're saying and I will take it into consideration. I'm not saying that you're right, but maybe you aren't wrong either. Maybe the truth is somewhere in the middle. But for right now, I need you to realize that your sister was very close to being right there with Carl Anderson, and had that happened, it would have directly resulted from you choosing to go off and get high rather than watch your sister. You can be mad at me all you want for what you think

I'm doing wrong, but that doesn't change the fact that our family dodged a bullet tonight. We're all gonna sit down and think long and hard about this and we're gonna have a talk real soon. In the meantime, if I so much as *think* you smoked pot again, you're gonna regret the day you first laid your lips on a drug. You understand me?"

"Yes."

Jack looked in the rearview mirror at his daughter. Quiet in the backseat, she held her mother's elf while tears streamed silently down her cheeks.

Jack Feltcher thought about his kids. He thought about his dead wife. And then his heart ached for only a moment longer before his brain steered him back toward finances.

Something had to give. Jack wasn't sure what that something would be.

The moment they arrived home, Jack sent the kids to bed. After Katy returned from work, she went straight upstairs to her room, wanting no part of Jack after the events that had transpired earlier. Once he'd given his children sufficient time to perform their bedtime routines, he popped into their respective bedrooms to check on them.

The two oldest were fast asleep while Cindy wept silently in her bed. Jack went to his daughter, sitting on the edge of the bed.

"Honey, I know what you saw today was tough. If you need to talk to Daddy, you can tell me anything."

Cindy shook her head and explained to her father she wasn't crying about Carl. The grisly scene had upset her, but she was crying about Jonesy. It had been a few days since he'd last come home.

Her admission threw Jack off guard. He couldn't believe

that she was more upset over the damn cat than the gruesome murder of a classmate.

So Jack did all he could think of to do in the moment—he lied. "Jonesy will be okay," he said. "He's a smart cat. If he got out, he will make his way back. Maybe he's hanging out with his kitty girlfriend." The moment the words left his lips, he realized how stupid they sounded.

If Jonesy had been missing for a few days because he'd somehow escaped, he most certainly wouldn't be okay. There were coyotes in the area at night, and Jonesy was an indoor cat. It was unlikely he could survive when the weather was nice, never mind during the harsh Southern New England winter they'd been experiencing.

If she knew he was lying, Cindy kept it to herself. Thank God for minor miracles.

"Get some sleep," he said to his daughter as he tucked her in.

Once he was sure the kids were all asleep, Jack rooted through the standalone freezer, searching for his bottle of Jack Daniel's. He kept it stashed in the bottom of the freezer because the kids stayed clear of the one in the back of the house. All of the food and desserts they liked were kept in the freezer in the kitchen. This was where Jack kept meats and other perishables. Since Courtney passed, he always kept a stash bottle lying around for those evenings he couldn't make it to a bar. Money wasn't his only addiction. Alcohol had been ruling his life for a few months now. And though he was sure the kids knew he drank—they were young, not stupid—he didn't think they knew he was what some people would call a functioning alcoholic. He didn't realize it himself until only recently.

Alcoholism aside, if Jack had been a sober man, today's events would have called for a drink. At the bar, he typically pounded shots and beers. But he was home tonight, not at the bar, so he figured he might as well put a little effort into making a tasty drink. Something seasonal, like a Very Merry Eggnog—Jack Daniel's with eggnog, cinnamon, and nutmeg. It sounded like just the thing he needed to fix the Christmas disaster this season was turning out to be.

Jack slammed the freezer door shut. The bottle was missing. It had to be either Katy or Adam. Cindy was too young, or so he hoped. It could be either of the two older kids. Katy had become something of a rebel, and Adam had been dabbling in marijuana. He wasn't a firm believer that weed was the slippery slope to the hard shit that the War on Drugs told everyone, but he thought if his son was smoking, it wasn't a stretch for him to be a drinker too. The more Jack thought about it, the more this smelled like Adam's stupidity. Katy would have been smart enough to have someone buy the alcohol for her, and if she *had* drank Jack's alcohol, she certainly wouldn't have been stupid enough to drink the whole thing and then get rid of the bottle.

"Fucking Adam," Jack said, "the little bastard is going to get what's coming to him."

But Jack would save that for another night. He was ready to explode as it was, and waking up his son in the middle of the night for a confrontation when he was seething was nothing more than a recipe for disaster.

CHAPTER ELEVEN

The Feltcher siblings once again sat in the basement, their hangout of choice. When their mother had been alive, they stuck to their bedrooms. But with her passing and Jack's absence, it was like they subconsciously flocked to the comfort of each other's presence.

Christmas movies played on the television while the three of them enjoyed takeout from their favorite spot, China Fun. Cindy clutched a fork in one hand and the elf in her other. It seemed the toy hadn't left her side since the night she found it.

Adam chewed his sweet and sour chicken and stared at his younger sister with a look of disgust plastered across his face. "Why don't you put that thing down while you eat? It's gross. Imagine the germs all over that thing. Look how dirty it is," Adam said.

Cindy looked at her brother. "*His* name is Sprinkles. And he is a *he*, not an it."

"Yeah, you've said that before. Not that I give a shit, but why would you name that thing Sprinkles. People *like* Sprinkles. On their ice cream, on their donuts, on their cake. *Nobody* likes that dirty ass thing but you."

Katy snorted, spitting out a bit of the Coke she'd been sipping on.

"I didn't name him Sprinkles. That's his name. He *told* me. And you know what else he told me? He told me you're a little bitch."

Cindy's face flushed. She'd surprised herself with the comment. But she wasn't lying. Sprinkles *did* tell her that. The night she'd found Carl Anderson dying in the snow, she'd had a dream Sprinkles could talk. He had a lot to say. Cindy knew Sprinkles couldn't talk in real life, but she did believe that her mother's spirit used Sprinkles to speak with her in her dreams.

Cindy thought it was sad her mother spoke about Adam like that. Maybe something got mixed up in the dream. Or maybe she'd been watching from Heaven and was disappointed with her son's behavior.

"You know what? I was just being an asshole, but I'll tell you what. You're twelve years old. You're old enough to know that imaginary friends are little kid shit. So I'm gonna take that shitty fucking elf and I'm going to get rid of it. If you want to run your mouth, at least don't blame it on a damn toy."

Adam jumped up and stormed toward Cindy, snatching the elf from her clutches.

"Adam, wait a minute," Katy said.

"No way. She's not gonna talk to me like that, and clearly this thing has turned her brain to mush."

Cindy cried, screaming hysterically.

Katy stood up, stepped, and blocked Adam's pursuit. "Just wait a minute, she's been through a lot."

"Yeah, and she needs therapy, not an imaginary friend." Adam pushed Katy out of the way, ran up the steps.

Cindy couldn't believe what a jerk her brother was. And why didn't Katy do more to stop him? Katy was eighteen, she was an adult. She could have *made* him give Sprinkles back.

The back door slammed shut, and a few minutes later Cindy heard it creak open again before slamming shut one last time.

Adam stomped down the steps and sat back down, picking up his food and continuing to eat as if nothing had happened.

"Wh-where . . . did you . . . p-put . . . Sprinkles?" Cindy asked, stuttering the words out with tears still streaming down her face.

"In the garbage where it belongs. And if I see that thing in this house again, I'm gonna throw it in the fireplace."

"I hate you. I wish you were the one that died," Cindy said as she ran up the basement stairs."

Katy looked at Adam and shook her head. She placed her food on the table and followed Cindy.

CHAPTER TWELVE

Christmas Eve morning had arrived and Sandra Kettle lay sprawled on her bed. With her legs splayed apart, she plunged an eight-inch purple dildo into her vagina, moaning from waves of pleasure as the toy cock slid in and out. With her free hand, she kneaded her breasts and played with her nipples. She wriggled on the bed, moaning as she fucked herself, soaking the sheets with her own juices. Sandra longed for the weight and warmth of a real cock in her pussy, but she was forced to change her plans when the escort service informed her that her "boyfriend for the evening" had canceled. She'd been disappointed at first. Real dick was usually better, so long as the man attached to it knew how to fuck, but Sandra could take care of herself when the need arose.

She fucked herself deeper and harder, rubbing her clitoris now instead of her breast. Her moans grew more guttural, animalistic, as she approached her second climax.

A pounding noise at her front door broke her concentration, and she lost her orgasm. Frustrated, Sandra tried to block out the noise, focusing on the growing warmth spreading throughout her stomach and pubic area. She had been so close to finishing, but sometimes when losing an orgasm, it could be difficult to get back to that point. She might need to take a break and try again later. Hopefully, that wasn't the case.

Sandra kept at it but before she could get a good rhythm going again, her doorbell camera went off. "What the fuck?" She tossed her dildo onto the bed and reached over to the nightstand for her phone. Tapping the screen, she opened the app and monitored the live feed.

Standing on her porch was a man in a Santa costume, complete with a large red sack and a long, fake beard. Now she was confused. The escort service definitely told her the appointment had been canceled. Had they not communicated that to their employee?

She pressed the **<PUSH-TO-TALK>** button. "I thought you guys weren't sending anyone out? The agency said my appointment was canceled."

On the screen, she saw Santa staring into the doorbell camera. He had a look of surprise on his face, like he had never seen one before. The man cleared his throat and spoke, "Umm, no. They never mentioned a cancellation to me. Maybe they were talking about later appointments when the storm gets worse?"

"Okay, give me a minute, please," she said.

Why was it so hard to find good customer service? How hard was it to give your customers the correct information? It didn't matter anymore, anyway. She was horny as hell and at least the interruption had been worth it. She wouldn't need the purple cock now. She had a real deal stud standing on her doorstep. A man whose dick game was so good he got paid to use it. She thanked God every day that her coworker, Janice, had told her about the escort service. Tinder had been a huge failure. Nothing but low-life liars and assholes who were using the service to cheat on their wives. She'd much rather pay a man to fuck her brains out and leave than navigate the scummy waters of online dating.

Sandra absentmindedly rubbed her thighs together. There would be no pillow talk or foreplay here. Santa was a stunt cock for the night, nothing more. She'd paid for an hour of time, but with how worked up she was, it wouldn't take half that long.

Sandra threw her shorts on and slipped into her favorite Krampus T-shirt as she walked toward the front door. Before opening it, she stopped to pull her shirt down, making sure her breasts stretched the thin cotton for all it could handle. Satisfied, she opened the door with a predatory grin.

The man in the Santa costume was tall with a slightly muscular build, though in the suit it was hard to tell for sure. The suit looked worse for wear, had definitely seen better days. But then again, it was likely nothing more than a seasonal prop. Sandra wondered how many women liked to get railed by a man roleplaying as Santa Claus. Probably not many. She was one of only two women she knew to use an escort service. It probably wasn't worth it for her date to spend too much money on caring for the costume or replacing it when needed.

"C'mon in, stud," she said.

"You're the boss."

"No, I don't like that. I'm not a domme. Come with me and close the door. It's cold outside." Sandra giggled. "You know, I didn't expect to be draining Santa's sack today."

Santa practically choked when he heard the words escape her lips. He recovered quickly, though, and Sandra was so horny she didn't notice the slipup. He closed the door and followed Sandra, his stiff johnson pressed against his red pants as he watched her ass jiggle with each step.

"What's that woman say in the movie, 'Fuck me, Santa'?" Sandra asked as she pulled her black T-shirt over her head, her large breasts partially visible from behind. She stepped out of her shorts and flicked them aside with a snap of her foot before turning around and bending over her bed.

Chad tore his costume off faster than he'd ever removed a piece of clothing in his life. He wasn't about to let this opportunity slip by. Not after all the time he'd spent in prison imagining what it felt like to be with a woman. He remembered hearing a song on the MP3 player he'd inherited from his cellmate when the man had been granted parole. Something about a "wet-ass pussy." At the time, he had thought it was a bit of a silly song, but now, with a real live, wet-ass pussy bent over in front of him, there was nothing silly about it.

Chad licked his hand and rubbed his shaft more out of habit than necessity before guiding his cock into Sandra's wet vagina.

The sensation of a warm, pulsating cock inside her, rather than her toy, heightened her arousal to where she was almost back to where she left off before the interruption. His dick was not as big as she had hoped—they rarely were—but it was *just* thick enough to take her to the promised land if she focused. That was okay, Sandra was used to that. Most men really didn't know what the hell they were doing anyway, and it required heavy mental focus on her part in order to achieve her orgasm and avoid battering the fragile male ego.

"Fuck me, Santa. Fuck me, Santa. Fuck me, Santa," Sandra repeated.

Chad obliged, pounding away from behind while Sandra backed up into him. The meaty slap of thighs on ass cheeks filled the room, along with the scent of sweat and her musk.

Santa's moans grew louder as he held her hips in a tight grip, his fingernails raking her skin. She winced, biting her lip. But it was a good pain so she wouldn't complain. Sandra could sense his impending climax, the sound of his fevered grunts and the increasing intensity of each thrust telling her she'd need to finish soon or she wouldn't finish at all. *I can't believe they sent me a two pump chump.*

Not willing to risk losing another orgasm, Sandra pulled away from the thrusting Saint Nicholas. She pushed him back gently. Lying back on the bed, she spread her legs, exposing her glistening sex. "Slow down," she said. "I need to come too. First me, then you."

She scooted forward, allowing her legs to hang over the edge of the bed. Only her upper torso lay on the mattress. Santa stepped in close, threw her legs over his shoulders, and started pumping away once more. Each thrust felt harder and deeper. Sandra was almost there.

"Oh, Santa!" she cried out.

"My name is Chad," he said.

The comment threw Sandra off. Of course he wasn't Santa. She wasn't a fucking moron. But if you're going to show up to fuck someone in a Santa costume, you could at least stay in character.

"Shut up, you idiot. I want you to fuck me. And you can choke me while you do it. Don't talk. Just. Fuck," she said, each slap of his thighs punctuating the words that came out of her mouth.

She closed her eyes, reached down, and rubbed her clit. Chad leaned forward and placed one hand on her neck, putting pressure on her carotid artery. He squeezed. As he did so, he noticed the huge purple dong a few feet away. A grin crept across his face and he applied a bit more pressure as he leaned forward to grab the dildo.

Here it was, that warm feeling growing, expanding from her genitalia throughout her body. Waves of pleasure rocked her, sent her to the stars. She cried out, "Fuck, I'm coming, I'm coming, I'm—"

Chad rammed the huge, purple pecker into her mouth. Her teeth scraped the thick, rubber cock and, after only a few inches of penetration, caught in place. The girth was too much for her.

Sandra's eyes bulged. Her jaw felt as if it were unhinging.

She clawed at Chad, fighting to stop him while struggling to breathe, but he was too strong. Her nails tore at his forearms, streams of blood trickling down toward his wrists.

"You bitch," he said and punched the scrotal base of the dildo, ramming the sex toy a few inches deeper.

Strained noise escaped her throat but nothing more. As Chad continued humping away, Sandra's attempts to defend herself grew weaker, feeble. Her chest burned, her temples throbbed. Tears blurred her vision and the last thing she saw before losing consciousness was Chad tossing his head back in ecstasy as he achieved the orgasm she'd been denied.

Chad stepped out of her, his seed spent and his cock already shrinking. "Don't call me a fucking idiot," he said.

Chad went to the bathroom and washed up, taking his time in the steamy shower. It had been some time since he'd last enjoyed the luxury of a nice wash. Once Christmas Eve was over, Chad fully expected to be dead or in the back of a police cruiser. With the coming blizzard and Sandra—the Feltcher family's only neighbor—out of the way, Chad had more than enough time to ruin Officer Jack Feltcher's Christmas.

CHAPTER THIRTEEN

Christmas Eve morning came and went with little fanfare in the Feltcher household. Jack left for work before the sun rose, the kids all fast asleep. Jack was the only morning person in the house.

Things had been tense between everyone since Christmas break started, before that really, but now, you could cut that tension with a knife.

Jack had laid into Adam about both the missing alcohol—which Adam claimed to have no knowledge of—and tossing Sprinkles in the garbage.

Sprinkles had been missing since that night. Katy had gone to retrieve the elf from the trash, ignoring Adam's threats, but Sprinkles was nowhere to be found. The elf was MIA, just like Jonesy. Of course Adam denied being responsible for the disappearance of Sprinkles, but nobody in the house believed him.

A few hours after Jack left for work, the siblings filtered their way downstairs in various states of wakefulness. Despite the tensions of recent days, Katy and Cindy cooked breakfast for the three of them while Adam set the table and brewed coffee for himself and Katy. He poured a glass of apple juice for Cindy.

After they'd eaten their breakfast, the Feltcher siblings made their way to the basement to watch the day-long marathon of *A Christmas Story.* Cindy hated the movie. It was a classic, sure, but at twelve years old the movie was simply *too* old for her to enjoy. It was like school reading assignments. They wanted you to read the same "classics" that had been taught in school for the last forty or fifty years and wondered why most of the kids loathed reading. For Cindy, watching the movie was more borne from tradition passed on by her mother, as were most Feltcher holiday traditions. Dad clearly had no intention of keeping the family traditions alive, so Cindy felt that duty rested upon her shoulders.

Katy and Adam watched with her, though she knew they hated the movie, too, and were likely watching it out of habit. Or maybe they were trying to keep the peace. She couldn't be sure.

After the movie played, they'd move on to other, more modern holiday movies. *Home Alone, Elf, How the Grinch Stole Christmas, Die Hard, Gremlins,* and even *Krampus.* Those were the *real* classics. Cindy hoped maybe this year Katy and Adam would let her watch a few of the more mature Christmas horror movies. She wasn't a huge horror fan by any means, but she did like a good scare now and then, and something about Christmas horror just hit differently.

Adam was the first to break the silence they'd been drowning in. "Listen, Cindy, about the other night. I'm sorry. I overreacted, but I really didn't take your elf from the garbage. I don't know where he went."

Cindy bit her lip, trying to think of what to say. She'd already talked about this at length with Katy. Nobody else was home. If he didn't take Sprinkles from the garbage, then it meant he never put Sprinkles there in the first place. Did he really think she was stupid enough to believe that? Sprinkles talked to her, yeah, but that was in her dreams. He couldn't talk for real. The only speech Sprinkles was capable of was nothing more than pre-recorded phrases on a voice box. Things like "Hi, I'm Sprinkles, wanna play? And "You're on the nice list, aren't you?"

"Adam, I'm not stupid. If you didn't take him out of the garbage, then you never put him there. You hid him somewhere else. Either way, I don't want to talk about it. If you're not gonna tell me where you put him, then just stop talking about it. He was Mom's and now I have one less thing to remember her by."

"Whatever. I'm not lying. I tried to be nice, but you're being ridiculous. If I did something to the damn thing, I'd tell you about it. I didn't touch that disgusting thing, but I hope wherever it is, someone was smart enough to torch it."

"You know what? Why don't both of you cut the shit? It's Christmas Eve and once again, all we have are the three of us. Not today. Please," said Katy.

Cindy and Adam both had no response for Katy. No smart remarks. She was right, and for once, she showed the wisdom that came with being a few years older than her siblings.

Katy snickered and then burst out laughing. "I'm just busting your chops. I don't give a shit if you argue all day long. Anyway, Jimmy is coming over for dinner tonight. Adam, you said Bobby was going to come by and hang out. What about you, Cindy? Dad said you could have a friend over if you had anyone that didn't need to be home early on Christmas morning," Katy said.

Cindy sighed.

She had asked no one. She didn't have many friends, and the few she had kept their distance once their mother had passed. They never said anything to her, but she eventually noticed that they always had reasons why they couldn't hang out or excuses why they'd excluded her from plans and events.

It was something she'd talked about with her therapist and the only thing they concluded was that maybe those friends didn't know how to be there for her after such a loss, and it made them uncomfortable. Cindy thought that was a load of crap. They were uncomfortable? She was the one with no mom, not them. Either way, she wasn't going to try to talk to the people who'd abandoned her when she most needed her friends.

"All of my friends would need to be home tonight or real early in the morning, so none of them can make it," Cindy said. She decided to give her sister a half-truth. No need to blow up her own spot and let Adam and Katy find out all of her friends had abandoned her when she needed them most. Much easier and less embarrassing to pretend they couldn't make it. Besides, even if her friends *hadn't* abandoned her, there was no way their parents would let them sleep over on Christmas Eve, so technically it wasn't a lie.

"Okay, well, is there anything you want to do tonight? Obviously we're gonna order Chinese again—that's one holiday tradition I'm never breaking—but was there anything else? Once Jimmy gets here, I'm gonna be hanging with him for a while, but he's gonna have to be a part of whatever festivities if he plans on sticking around for the evening," Katy said.

Cindy thought about it for a minute. Nothing really stuck out in her head that she just *had* to do tonight, though she thought it would be a good time to pitch those scary movies.

"I was thinking maybe this year we could watch some of the scarier Christmas movies. You know, stuff like *Silent Night?* And I'll bake more cookies. We have sooo much cookie dough in the fridge. I made sure to add a bunch to the cart when Dad was ordering the delivery. He doesn't know I have the login info." Cindy smiled at her own ability to pull a fast one over on their father.

Adam side-eyed Cindy. Katy laughed.

"Okay, I don't have a problem with that, but if you get nightmares, we're gonna tell Dad you snuck downstairs and watched them when we were sleeping," Katy said.

"Okay, deal!" Cindy's day was looking better already, although she did still miss Sprinkles and Jonesy.

Maybe there would be a Christmas Eve miracle and they'd both turn up.

Chad walked around Sandra Kettle's house, where he'd already spent a few hours napping. He'd shown up so early in the morning that he had most of an entire day to kill before heading across the street to exact his revenge. The rest was glorious, sleeping in such a nice bed, and he'd nosed about the house, enjoying himself before eventually he grew paranoid and realized he might have made a grave mistake. His plan had seemed genius at first. The house was the only other home near Officer Feltcher's and made a perfect stakeout post for him to monitor the Feltcher residence until it was time to make his move. He knew there was a nor'easter expected to decimate the area, and he also knew that Jack Feltcher typically worked holidays, despite having kids. The money was too good to turn down, and like most of the officers at the prison, money motivated Feltcher.

There was a potential problem, however.

Chad had done no research into the woman he'd killed. She'd been a victim of circumstance. Killing her would help things along later on. All he knew from prior recon was that she had a lot of visitors coming in and out of the house, but it appeared as if she lived alone. He'd done no digging into the woman, and even if he wanted to, he didn't have the means to conduct any sort of investigation. Hell, Chad didn't even know her name until he'd snooped through her belongings after killing her.

One thing that kept him on edge: was she expecting family tonight? She might have been, although the way she had confused Chad with someone else who she had apparently canceled an appointment with led him to believe she wasn't expecting anyone until at least later on in the day, if at all.

It was too late, though, to take back what had already been done. The wheels in motion couldn't be stopped. If someone showed up at the house, he would deal with them, plain and simple. Nothing would get in his way now.

Chad decided he'd keep her phone on him for the time being. There was no lock on it, so at least this way he'd be able to respond to text messages. And if it came down to it, buy himself some time if people began poking around.

He had high hopes for the rest of his Christmas plans. Phase one had gone off well enough. Better than he had hoped, really. If he hadn't been stupid enough to shoot his load inside the woman he'd just murdered, maybe he'd have even gotten away with that one. Not that it mattered. He wanted to go back to prison, but knowing he'd committed the vicious crime and gotten away with it would have been a nice feather in his cap.

Chad made his way to the front of the home, watching the snow fall and the wind whip while sipping a steaming cup of coffee he'd brewed in Sandra's kitchen. Bones Coffee. Not bad. He'd been living off of instant shit water they passed off as coffee in the prison commissary for so long that even the worst store-brand junk tasted better.

In the Feltcher's driveway, another vehicle was slowly coming to a stop. It wasn't either of Jack's vehicles, and it wasn't his daughter's vehicle.

Two people exited, one of them carrying a large plastic bag in each hand. It was difficult to tell, but from the shapes and sizes, Chad thought both were male. Who could they be, though? Family members? Friends? Chad would have to account for the unfamiliar faces when he sat down to plan exactly how he'd handle the rest of the night.

It was still early enough in the evening; Chad had plenty of time to prep for tonight's festivities. If he had to kill two more people, then he'd do exactly that. But for now, he thought he'd enjoy the amenities of his host's home. He suspected tonight would be his last night as a free man.

CHAPTER FOURTEEN

For the first time since Mom had died, the Feltcher siblings sat together at the dining table to enjoy their meal. Dad, as usual, wasn't present. They knew that would be the case. He was working at least a double, and they expected him to call home any minute now to let them know he wouldn't be home until sometime tomorrow. Still, it was Christmas Eve and despite everything they had been through that seemed to get worse as each day passed, everyone was excited. At the very least, they knew they were going to have some sweet gifts under the tree because Jack Feltcher, although absent from his kids' day-to-day lives, spared no monetary expense when it came to making his children happy.

Cindy only wished he was willing to spare a bit more of his time. That would really thrill her.

The evening almost hadn't been quite as delightful as they'd hoped, however. In full swing now, the nor'easter was giving the town of Glenwood and the rest of the state a brutal pounding. Katy called their favorite Chinese spot—who'd been seeing more and more of the Feltcher family's money since Courtney passed—only to be told that orders tonight would be pickup only, and the store would be closing at five p.m.

Katy had hung up the phone and given her brother and sister the bad news. Cindy begged Katy to pick up the food, but Katy wanted no part of driving around in the storm. Cindy was relentless, and eventually Katy agreed to order the food, but only if Jimmy was willing to pick up the order on his way over.

Jimmy agreed and was also kind enough to pick up Adam's friend, Bobby, on his way over.

Cindy didn't really care for Bobby. She thought he was a bit of a creep. He never said anything weird to her or touched her, but she didn't like the way he was always staring at Katy. She was only twelve, but she knew what those looks from boys meant.

At the table, Bobby belched and pushed his chair back, scraping the legs across the hardwood floor.

"Hey man, my dad is gonna fuck you up if you scratch the hardwood. Lift your damn chair, you animal," Adam said.

Bobby looked at Adam for a moment, his eyes low, red, and glossy from the weed he and Adam had smoked before they sat down to eat. He burst out laughing, rocking back and forth as if it were the funniest thing in the world to be asked to treat someone else's home with respect. "Yeah, man, like he gives a shit," Bobby said.

"It isn't funny, dumbass," Katy said. "If you keep this shit up, *I'm* gonna beat your ass. You won't have to wait for my dad to get home."

Bobby stopped laughing for the time being. "All right, all right. Chill out. I'll go easy on the floor next time."

Cindy rolled her eyes. Even she didn't believe that one. She took a bite of her egg roll and enjoyed the crunch, savored the delicious taste. China Fun had the best egg rolls around. They rarely ordered from a different spot, but the times they did, Cindy wouldn't bother with the egg rolls.

They didn't have the same crunch these did, and for her, the crunch made the roll. She dipped the roll into her sweet and sour sauce, a habit both Katy and Adam always heckled her about. She didn't care. The sauce was delicious, and dipping the roll in it was just a way to have more of it. They always gave you far too much sauce for the amount of chicken, and she had no idea why. They had to know at least half the sauce was going in the garbage.

"How's your food, Cindy?" Katy asked.

Cindy blushed and gave her sister a thumbs-up, embarrassed at the attention drawn to her while she had a mouthful of food. She chewed quickly and took a swig of her Pepsi, swallowing the rest of the chunks with the help of the cola. "How's yours?" Cindy asked.

"Good, I wish I had ordered more."

They were all creatures of habit, Cindy knew. She always ordered the sweet and sour chicken, Katy the General Tso, and Adam the orange chicken. All three of them always wished they'd ordered more. And they might have if Jimmy hadn't been the one to pay for the food. Cindy wasn't sure why Jimmy had paid. She didn't think there was anything going on between Katy and him, but who knew with people their age?

Bobby and Adam stood up together as if on cue. Adam punched Bobby's shoulder. "Let's go upstairs. I'm gonna beat your ass at *Madden*."

"Yeah, because I fucking hate football. How about you play me at *Valorant* and then you can talk shit."

"Nah, I don't play nerd shit like that."

"Because you suck."

"No, because I'm not a geek."

"Dude, you're the biggest fucking geek I know. Just because you're a pothead doesn't make you *not* a geek."

Their voices trailed off as they disappeared up the steps on their way to Adam's room.

Jimmy broke the silence. "So, uh, what should we do?"

"I don't know, Jimmy. What do you want to do?" Katy asked.

Okay, maybe there is *something going on with those two,* Cindy thought.

"Umm, watch Netflix?"

"Netflix? Wow, I thought you wanted to just hang out, didn't know you wanted to chill."

"Are you two kidding me? I'm almost thirteen. I know what the hell you mean by *Netflix and chill*. You guys are gross, Cindy said."

Jimmy blushed and pulled at his collar. "Hey, I'm not trying to do any of that, little girl. You got the wrong idea."

"Don't call me 'little girl,' my name is Cindy." She was already frustrated by Adam and Bobby heading upstairs to play games instead of watching a movie as they'd planned. And now Katy's friend was calling her a little girl, which further upset her. She *hated* when people called her that. In just a few months she'd be a teenager—there was nothing little about that! Maybe this night wasn't going to be as fun as she'd hoped. How quickly things change.

"He's right, Cindy. I'm the one being gross. Jimmy here couldn't read a signal if he had a decoder ring."

"If you want to tell the story the right way: I can read them just fine. I *choose* to ignore them."

It was Cindy's turn to scoot her chair back and excuse herself. "Well, you two do whatever it is you're gonna do. I'm going downstairs to watch movies. It would be nice if everyone didn't leave me by myself all night. Not on Christmas Eve." She felt tears welling up and her chin quivered.

"Hey, Jimmy, why don't you wait upstairs for me? I'm gonna talk to Cindy for a minute," Katy said.

"Yeah, okay. I got you."

Jimmy left the two sisters alone.

Katy walked over to where her sister stood, picking up the remains of her dinner. She put her hands on Cindy's shoulders. "Hey, kiddo, chill, ok? We aren't gonna be gone all night. It isn't like that with Jimmy. You're right, I *was* being gross, but Jimmy won't do anything. He's just here to hang out. We're gonna listen to music and talk for a bit, and then I promise we will eat all the cookies you told us you were gonna bake. Is that okay? We're gonna be up as late as we want watching movies. I just want one hour to talk with Jimmy. I kinda like him and he isn't into moving fast like that. Please?"

Cindy chewed her lip. She understood where Katy was coming from. She wasn't sure she believed Katy when she said there wasn't going to be any funny business, but there was no point in making a bigger fuss. If she did, Katy might go nuclear, flip her shit, and then leave Cindy to fend for herself the rest of the evening. She didn't want that to happen, not tonight. And the way Katy had behaved since their mother died, there was no way to tell how she'd react at any given time.

"Okay. But just one hour, right? I'll watch something downstairs for a bit, and then I'll put the cookies in the oven so they'll be ready to eat when it's time to watch movies."

"I promise, one hour."

"Okay."

Katy kissed her sister on the forehead and made her way toward the stairs. Cindy called out to her. "Hey, Katy?"

Katy spun around. "Yeah?"

"Don't call me 'kiddo' anymore, I'm almost a teenager."

Katy laughed. "Okay, whatever you say. One hour and we'll all head downstairs."

Cindy walked to the kitchen, tossing her trash in the garbage bin and her silverware in the sink before digging around in the cabinets for the cookie trays and parchment paper. She left everything set up and ready to go for when it was time to bake and made her way to the basement, stopping at the wicker basket in the hallway to grab a throw blanket.

Cindy took the stairs two at a time. Things hadn't gone according to plan, but the train wasn't derailed just yet. Hopefully, only delayed. And if nobody came downstairs, she decided it wasn't going to ruin her night. She was tired of letting other people get to her. It was Christmas Eve and nobody was going to put a damper on her having a jolly time.

Downstairs, she took up position in front of the television and wrapped herself in the throw. She scrolled through the VOD movies for a bit but couldn't settle on one.

"If they don't want to come down here, they don't get a say in what I watch," she said as she highlighted *Silent Night* and clicked the **<RENT>** button.

CHAPTER FIFTEEN

For the first time since losing his wife, Jack Feltcher experienced a moment of clarity strong enough to convince him to change his ways. Tonight he was going to break the cycle of acknowledging the negative impact his hours had on his family, while also claiming the overtime was a necessity. His children were right, there *was* a happy medium. He could easily take on extra hours while still being home more often for his children. Nobody was forcing him to work thirty-two-hour shifts. It was his own choice to work those extended shifts. He'd gotten addicted to money, but more importantly, he finally was ready to admit he used work as an escape.

So when the inevitable happened and the shift supervisor began calling on the radio for voluntary graveyard shift overtime, Jack surprised both his boss and coworkers by turning it down. No doubt that pissed someone off. Jack was a worker, and his unwillingness to take voluntary overtime meant that if they could not fill that spot on the roster, someone was going to be ordered into *involuntary* overtime on Christmas Eve. Jack felt bad at first, but he worked so much overtime, he did more than his fair share. Every day someone else got spared from an order over because he took the spot voluntarily. It was time for *him* to spend the evening with his family for once.

The only thing separating Jack and his children now were the last few remaining hours of his shift. He would go on his lunch break, return to work for the tail end of his shift, and then get the hell out of Dodge.

The drive home was sure to be hell; the storm was really doing a number on the entire state. He hoped the governor didn't call a state of emergency. If it got to that point, he could be held over onto the next shift even though he was already working a double. He didn't think it would come to that. They'd have to order over the entire second shift before they hit the guys who were already on overtime from the morning. But with the department's staffing crisis, you were never safe from involuntary overtime until you were driving out of the parking lot.

He hadn't told his kids yet for a few reasons. First and foremost, he didn't want to risk getting their hopes up, only to pull the rug from underneath them. His absence had caused them enough mental stress; Jack saw no need to add to it. Second, he wanted to surprise his children.

There was a part of him that knew they were older and didn't care to be around their old man as much, but there was another part of him—the part that would always see his three children as his babies—that longed to see a look of joy on their faces when he walked in the door to be with them. And last, there was the law enforcement part of him. The part he couldn't always pack away before he went home. It told him two teens and a preteen home alone overnight were up to no good, and it was up to him to catch them in the act.

Jack Feltcher told that part of his brain to shut the fuck up. This year, he was coming home for Christmas, and there wasn't a damn thing in the world that would ruin it.

CHAPTER SIXTEEN

Bobby cocked his arm back and was about to throw the PlayStation controller against the wall, but at the last second, he realized he was holding Adam's controller, not one of his own. He had zero tolerance when it came to losing at video games, even if it was a game he hated, like *Madden*. He didn't give a shit about sports, especially football. The only sport he could tolerate was basketball, and even then it was only something he did because most of his friends played. But a sport video game? To him, that seemed weird. Why not play the real thing?

So he bitched and moaned until finally Adam agreed to play *Dragon Ball FighterZ*. The game was old, and the name was horrible, but they were both fans of fighting games and anime, so it had lasting appeal for both of them. Although playing against Adam really brought out the worst in Bobby. He felt like he could mop the floor with anyone. But for whatever reason, no matter what game they played—except for *Valorant*—Bobby just couldn't get the upper hand. Adam was better at pretty much any game they played. As someone who considered himself an expert gamer, it was a hard pill to swallow.

"Hey man, don't break my shit. You know how expensive these damn controllers are now," Adam said.

"Yeah, I know. I almost did it for a second, kinda forgot we were at your house. You've seen the holes in my wall." Bobby laughed. There were quite a few holes decorating the walls in his bedroom. Various posters he'd hung up concealed the damage from his parents, which was the only reason he hadn't gotten his ass whooped yet. That would come, eventually.

"You wanna play something else?" Adam asked.

Bobby knew he'd put his friend in an awkward position. They were having fun playing video games, and his outburst had threatened to ruin a good time. He'd always had a temper, a product of living with a verbally and physically abusive father, and though he tried to keep it under control, sometimes he slipped, and the rage within him boiled over. Being around him during those times made his friends uncomfortable, even though he'd never been violent toward another living creature. But he knew during those times when he lost his cool, his buddies felt like it was only a matter of time before the target was another person.

After mulling it over, Bobby thought maybe they'd change it up, play something a bit more relaxing. "How about you play something on the PlayStation, and I'll play my Switch? I just bought the new Mario game, so we can just chill here and each play our own thing. Besides, I'm tired of getting my ass kicked."

"All right, if you don't mind. How is Mario, by the way? I never play the 2D ones anymore, but I keep hearing it's awesome."

"Bro, best game of the year. Honestly might be the best 2D Mario game since *World*, no cap."

"If you ever say 'no cap' in my house again, you're gonna be walking home in this blizzard, man. What's next, you gonna cut your hair like every other tool at school too?"

Bobby laughed. The comment instantly brought to mind the corny haircut that was in style now, some sort of weird amalgamation of a bowl haircut with wavy curls. "Nah, I was just being stupid, you know that. Man, that hairstyle is ridiculous. You ever seen that meme with Leonardo DiCaprio? It says 'Leonardo No Caprio.' I was high out of my mind the first time I saw it, almost choked to death on a *Cheeto.*"

"Yeah, I saw that one. It's a good meme."

Bobby pulled out his Switch and booted the game up. The nice thing about the console was it was so easy to take anywhere. Of course, the graphics weren't up to current standards. Hell, they weren't even up to current standards when the system was brand new. But when it came to fun, the machine had it in spades.

They played like that for a while—Bobby sprawled out on the floor, holding the console over his face and Adam plastered to his gaming chair, a contraption that looked like a computer chair and racing seat had a baby. In between levels, Bobby watched Adam web-swinging through the virtual New York metropolis. He'd have to order that one if his parents hadn't gotten it for him for Christmas.

Time slipped away, as it has a habit of doing when you're young and having fun. The blizzard rattled the windows in their frames, and the power had flickered a few times but was holding steady until Bobby jinxed them by acknowledging the flickering.

Blackness enveloped them, the only light coming from the OLED screen of Bobby's gaming console. "Give it a few. We have a whole house generator; it should kick on soon," Adam said.

A few minutes slipped by before Adam spoke again, "Well, I guess Dad forgot to swap the propane tank on the generator from the last storm."

"Propane? Your house runs on the same shit as my grill?"

"No, asshole. The generator runs on it. Most of the houses

in this part of town run on oil. We aren't connected to natural gas lines, so the only other option was propane."

"Seems like a shitty option to me."

"Well, usually it runs fine. But Dad is too busy with work and avoiding being home that he neglects to take care of shit like this."

"Right. Thanks for the science lesson. I'm gonna head outside and smoke a bowl. You wanna come?"

Adam thought about it for a minute before declining the invitation. "Nah, we still have to watch movies and shit with Cindy. I don't want to get that stoned around her."

"We were just high downstairs grubbing out on dinner not too long ago. But suit yourself. Play this while I'm gone, give yourself something to do," Bobby said as he handed the Switch to Adam.

"I might fuck around on TikTok, I don't feel like playing anything."

"Take a look at your phone, buddy," Bobby said. "You live out in the woods, man. You already know you don't get reception, and your Wi-Fi just went out with the power. You won't be doing shit on your phone."

The look of horror on Adam's face was hysterical. Like any kid their age, removing phone access was like removing oxygen from their lungs. For the moment, Bobby was laughing at Adam, but he knew it wouldn't be long before his Switch died and he was in the same boat.

With any luck, the weed would get him so high he wouldn't give a shit.

Feet up in the La-Z-Boy recliner, Chad was enjoying the creature comforts he'd missed out on while being locked up for so long. Tens of thousands of movies and television programs at your fingertips with a few taps of a remote. It took him a bit to get used to navigating the menus, but once he did, the sheer number of choices overwhelmed him. He found himself mindlessly scrolling through seemingly endless amounts of content until finally, he closed his eyes and picked something at random. Much easier than filtering through everything and deciding on his own.

Chad thought he could get used to living like this. But he knew he wouldn't get a chance to. This life wasn't for him. He was already resigned to his fate—he'd killed two people since getting out of prison. If he stopped right now, it changed nothing. He still had a one-way ticket to Glenwood Correctional Institute.

Halfway through the movie—some zombie flick—the power cut out.

It was time to finish this.

He pushed the recliner down, hopped off the chair. No more waiting for the perfect moment to strike. It had arrived. The storm was raging; the power was out. If this wasn't the universe telling him to strike while the iron was hot, he didn't know what would be.

Chad grabbed the large kitchen knife he'd placed on the coffee table and exited Sandra Kettle's home. He crossed the street, not bothering to shut the front door behind him.

CHAPTER SEVENTEEN

B obby stood on the back porch shivering, braving the elements to get stoned. The moment he stepped foot out the door, he realized his own stupidity. The storm was far too strong to make smoking a bowl feasible. He ran back inside to grab his jacket and swap the bowl for his weed pen.

He decided to smoke the pen on the porch out of respect for Adam's younger sister. Well, not really out of respect for her, it was because her father was a correction officer, and Bobby didn't trust her not to rat. He knew Jack Feltcher would blow the whole thing out of proportion if he knew someone was getting high at his house. Weed was legal now, but Feltcher still had the old law enforcement mentality about stuff like that.

He bounced up and down, hoping the movement would keep him warm. The wind whipped around tendrils of snow and ice that stung exposed skin. A couple more hits off the pen and he'd be finished outside.

The Feltcher family had decided they were all going to watch movies in the basement tonight. Bobby didn't want to watch anything, but if it meant he could spend time with

Adam's fine-ass older sister, Katy, he'd sit through any movie they put on. Part of the reason he'd agreed to come over tonight was to be around her. Something about her got him going, and he'd had fun dreams about her on more than one occasion. Sometimes he wished Adam wasn't a friend, then he could put the moves on Katy. But he couldn't do that to Adam, they were like brothers. Situations like that ruined friendships.

When Adam texted him Jimmy would be by to pick him up, he'd almost canceled. Bobby hadn't expected Katy to have some dude over. For as good-looking as Katy Feltcher was, she seemed to never have a boyfriend, never seemed to have any love interests or flings. He used to think it was because of their father's reputation for being a dickhead, but as he'd gotten to know the family better, especially since their mother passed, he realized it wasn't Jack Feltcher scaring the guys away; it was Katy Feltcher's personality. She was a miserable person to be around and made it a point to push everyone away. Fine by Bobby. Less competition.

Thinking about Katy caused a stir in his pants and his jeans grew tighter as his penis swelled with blood and lust. Maybe because he was stoned, or maybe because he was a weirdo, but he decided it would be a fun idea to go up the steps to the second floor deck and take a peek through Katy's window. If she and her new boyfriend were boning up there, it was possible he would see Jimmy's cock, but it stood to reason seeing Jimmy's cock brought a good chance of seeing Katy naked. Bobby thought the trade-off was worthwhile. With all the porn he'd watched, it wouldn't be the first cock he'd seen, and it definitely wouldn't be the last.

Did that make him a cuck? Bobby didn't think so. A voyeur for sure, but as long as it wasn't his girlfriend getting dicked down, he was safe from cuckdom. Or so he hoped.

The wind buffeted Chad, burning his cheeks and stinging his eyes. Between the sheets of snow flying around and how blurry his eyes had become from being assaulted by the precipitation, he could hardly see a thing. He'd only been outside three minutes, give or take, but he wasn't sure how much longer he could remain exposed to the elements. The threadbare Santa costume he'd stolen from the hobo wasn't doing a good job of keeping him warm, and it was already sopping wet. Once he was finished he'd have to steal some of Jack's clothes. Otherwise, the exposure might kill him.

He cursed himself for waiting as long as he did. The smart move would have been to head across the street as soon as he'd killed the bitch. But Chad hadn't been thinking clearly; he had been in a postorgasmic haze and enjoying luxuries he'd never see again. Now, he had to hope he'd finish the job before the weather finished him.

Once he'd reached the Feltcher's property, Chad crept along the driveway, using the knife he'd taken from across the street to punch the air from the tires of both vehicles. The noise was much louder than he'd expected. Luckily, the raging storm dampened the sound of everything. No way anyone would hear it from inside the house.

Past the driveway, Chad trudged through the mounds of snow along the side of the house. He kept his body against the home, that way anyone looking out a window would be less likely to see him.

A few feet from the house, Chad spied a small structure covering stacks of firewood. The tarp was thrown off the wood. Whoever had stacked the logs hadn't covered them. Either too lazy or too stupid to finish the final part of the job. Leaning against the wood was an axe, which Chad crossed the yard and retrieved. It appeared to be in almost brand-new condition and would come in handy for the festivities of the evening.

Chad ran back to the house and walked to the edge to scope the rear of the property.

Peeking around the corner of the house, Chad saw a young man, maybe a teenager, walking up the steps to the second floor of the deck. He wasn't sure if it was the Feltcher boy or one of the two males who'd shown up earlier. Although from the way they seemed to sneak up the stairs, if Chad were a betting man, he'd place his money on one of the newcomers.

No matter. Whoever it was, he'd handle it.

He moved quickly, closing the distance in a few strides, not worried about the person hearing him. Not with the wind howling the way it was. He dropped the axe and with his left hand, he grabbed the collar of the person's jacket, stopping their progress and pulling them backward. With his right hand, he pulled the kitchen knife from his belt and rammed it forward, the blade meeting the falling person as gravity helped punch it home.

The knife plunged into Bobby's back, easily slicing through the jacket and piercing flesh. The edge cut through fat and muscle, hitting the spinal cord. Bobby tried to scream but the moment he opened his mouth Chad put his hand over his face, muffling the teen's cry.

Chad guided the boy to the ground, removing the knife from his back as he did so. With serpentlike speed, he plunged the knife into the boy's chest, striking five times in quick succession. Like a chef carving a Christmas dinner ham, the blade sliced through Bobby's vital organs. Blood leaked from the holes in the jacket, pooling beneath the boy, staining the snow scarlet. The veins in Bobby's neck bulged and blood bubbled from one of the holes in his chest.

Chad had seen pictures of Feltcher's children at the prison. Jack Feltcher had been one of those dumb bastards who left personal items like family photos and knickknacks lying around on his desk, complacent to the fact that he was allowing inmates a glimpse into his personal life.

His initial observation had been correct, the boy was no Feltcher. Possibly a friend of one of the kids or some other relative. Either way, he'd spent enough time on someone who was nothing more than collateral damage. As much as he enjoyed the feeling of ripping someone's life from them, he wanted to end this one quickly so he could take care of Feltcher's children.

Chad ran the blade across Bobby's throat. A line appeared along his neck like a crimson smile. A moment after the grotesque grin appeared, blood gushed from the wound and Bobby bled out quickly.

Chad slipped the knife into his belt and took the steps he'd pulled the boy off of. It was time to see why he was sneaking around up there.

CHAPTER EIGHTEEN

The chirp of the radio cut through the silence. "Officer Feltcher," the voice said, "three hours holiday off?"

Jack couldn't believe it. Not only was he not getting ordered over, but they were letting people leave a few hours early—paid—for the holiday. How could he turn that down?

Jack replied, "10-4, I'll take it."

The radio crackled once more. "Roger that. Have the utility officer relieve you. Merry Christmas, and be careful on the roads."

Jack packed up his things and handed over the keys and handcuffs to the relieving officer. "Merry Christmas, brother. I'll see you in a few days," Jack said.

Officer Jackman laughed. "Must be nice to go home, ya bastard."

"Kid, get some time on the job then you'll have the seniority to do the same thing."

"Ayyy, always the seniority shit. I know, my punk five years is nothing in this place. Have a good night, man."

Jack nodded and made his way out of the building. The walk was long and cold. He had to walk through the yard to get to the other side of the building where the main foyer led to the parking lot. He stopped at his locker and retrieved his cell phone and car keys, using his remote starter to warm the vehicle. With any luck, by the time he hit the lot the defrosters would have done enough of a job that the snow and ice would be easy to clear from his windshield and windows.

He checked his phone, no service. The storm must have done something to the cell towers. Oh well, he'd surprise the kids like he originally planned, anyway. They'd definitely be up at this hour.

He walked to his car, smiling. For the first time since his wife died, Jack Feltcher knew his family would weather the storm.

CHAPTER NINETEEN

Adam waited a bit after Bobby left the room before grabbing his Switch. Once satisfied the coast was clear, he nabbed it from the bed. Bobby didn't care if he used it; he'd offered the thing to him. The reason he'd waited was simple: he didn't want to admit to Bobby he'd been right when he suggested Adam would get bored so soon without internet access. Adam's family and friends called him a know-it-all. They tossed the term around like it was an ugly word, something to be ashamed of. But the thing was: while Adam didn't know *everything* (that notion was absurd), he often *was* right about things, so much so it was a fact he took pride in. The very same fact annoyed the people around him to no end.

Some called it smug. He didn't know what to call it. All he knew was that it pissed him off far more than it should those few times he really *had* been wrong.

There was another thing Bobby had been right about. The new Mario game really was phenomenal. He'd made a new save file and started running and jumping through the levels, making it a point to collect every extra item on each stage and hit the top of the flagpole at the end of the levels. For the most part, it wasn't too difficult, but there were some stages he had to replay multiple times and *still* wasn't able to 100% them.

After playing for about twenty minutes, Adam placed the game console back where Bobby had left it. He would be back any second now. Adam picked his phone up before remembering the Wi-Fi was down. "Motherfucker," he said. "Where the hell is Bobby? It doesn't take this long to get high."

Adam knew Bobby could be a bit of a space cadet, prone to spacing out and showing up late for things because he was so stoned he'd simply forgotten. But something seemed off. He'd only gone downstairs; what could he have possibly gotten sidetracked with? The condition outside was far too brutal for him to brave the elements for this long. If anything, Bobby would have finished up as soon as possible and hit the kitchen to scrounge for something to quell the munchies, a task that shouldn't take more than a few minutes.

Maybe he was pestering Katy. Adam knew his best friend had the hots for his sister. Something that made Adam incredibly uncomfortable, especially because she was aware of it as well, and would tease him about hooking up with Bobby, thereby ruining his life. Or was he watching movies with Cindy? Had she come upstairs looking for someone to watch a movie with her like they'd all promised? It was certainly a possibility. They'd all agreed upon an hour of chill time before movie night and it had been about an hour longer than that. The more Adam thought about it, the more he realized that was the most likely scenario. Bobby wouldn't want to watch movies with Cindy if nobody else was around, but the prospect of baked goods and popcorn would be too alluring for his stoned mind to turn down.

Adam slid into his memory foam slippers and exited his bedroom, using his phone as a flashlight. As he walked down the hall, he heard a faint hum and the power kicked back on. The lights flickered a bit before holding steady. Talk about lucky. Now he could pocket his phone and not have to worry about draining the battery. He took the stairs two at a time, no longer worried about stumbling in the dark.

He did a little jump off the bottom step, his hand on the railing as he spun around the corner. Bobby was nowhere to be seen. The aroma of burning firewood permeated the first floor. Adam stopped and breathed deep. He loved having a working fireplace. It was one of his favorite things about the season. Sitting by the fire's warm glow, basking in the aroma, a mug of hot cocoa in hand. Unsure if anyone had checked on the fire recently, Adam went for a look.

He entered the living room, its large bay window blocked by a huge pine tree. Every year they made it a point to pick out a massive tree. One thing the Feltcher family always agreed on, the bigger the tree, the better. There was something special about having an actual tree rather than a fake version. The only downside was cleaning up the pine needles as the tree slowly died. Having Jonesy in the house meant they had to sweep often because if he were to eat them, they could pierce internal organs. It seemed a bit much, but owning a pet was a bit much no matter how you looked at it. So many things could kill or harm a pet, what was one more danger?

Lit up once more with the return of the power, the tree was beautiful. The flashing multicolored lights, the garland, the extravagant store-bought ornaments, and the sentimental handcrafted ornaments from when the children had been young—they all came together beautifully.

After staring at the tree for a bit, Adam remembered what he had come in for: the fire—it definitely needed some more wood. The fire had died down quite a bit and the hot glow could barely be considered warm at the moment. Adam picked up the poker and moved the wood around before placing another few pieces of wood in the firebox. Flames licked the fresh wood as it cracked and popped.

Adam cocked his head to the side. There was a rustling

noise coming from the top of the chimney. It stopped, and for a moment there was no further noise. But after a few moments of silence came a soft thump and then the rustling noise again. It grew louder, closer.

Did an animal get in the chimney?

Something large fell into the firebox, scattering the wood. Sparks flew out and Adam jumped back.

What the fuck?

It was Jonesy! The cat was clearly dead, no doubt about it. The orange fur was stained a dark red, but the fur was still wet and blood leaked from its body. Jonesy's eyes were missing; two empty, bleeding sockets decorated the cat's face. Jutting from the feline's side, two large kitchen knives.

Before Adam had a chance to scream, there was another thump from the chimney, followed by more rustling within. Something else was on the way down. A high-pitched squeal echoed inside the fireplace.

With a thump, something green landed on Jonesy. It rolled out of the fire, grasping the kitchen knives and taking Jonesy along for the ride. It whipped its arms out ahead of it, the momentum causing the cat's body to come loose from the knives. Jonesy flew across the room. Adam sidestepped the cat's corpse, the body landing where Adam had been standing. The cat's lifeless body rolled across the carpet, extinguishing the small flame spreading along its fur.

Sprinkles the elf brushed soot and embers off his tunic with his free hand, clutching the pair of knives in the other. "You almost roasted my nuts over an open fire, Adam!" Sprinkles said, cackling maniacally. "Speaking of nuts, how's your junk doing, little buddy? I wanted to chomp your little pecker right off but the nutcracker's teeth weren't quite sharp enough. I wonder if mine are. Won't ya give yer ole pal Sprinkles a bite?"

"I've gotta be hallucinating. Bobby must have put shrooms or some shit in my food."

Sprinkles tilted his head to the side, his soulless, grey eyes unblinking. "Who's Bobby? Sounds like he knows how to party." Sprinkles grinned ear to ear, opening his mouth and showing a maw full of sharklike teeth. Adam didn't remember the elf's teeth looking like that before. "Let me get a bite of your pecker, Adam. Don't make me ask again!" Sprinkles growled.

Adam backed up and tripped over Jonesy. Sprinkles stalked forward, opening and closing his mouth, clacking his teeth together with each step he took, threatening Adam with the impending loss of his manhood. Sprinkles slid the knives against each other, back and forth like a chef about to go to work.

Adam scrambled onto his hands and knees, but as he darted forward, Sprinkles slashed outward, one of the knives slicing Adam's Achilles tendon. He cried out and fell to the ground, clutching his heel.

Sprinkles slammed a knife into the top of Adam's foot, pinning it to the ground. Blood splashed from the wound. Adam howled. He tried to pull his foot up, but he felt something tear and quickly gave up. The pain was too much. He couldn't bring himself to rip his foot free. Sprinkles raised the second knife over his head and slammed it into Adam's other foot. Both feet were pinned to the ground now, blood leaking from each impaled foot, drenching the carpet.

Adam rocked back and forth on the floor, screaming, crying. He puked, chunks of chicken and egg roll splattering his chest.

Sprinkles snapped his fingers and a stocking materialized in his hands. He looked in the top of the stocking and wrinkled his nose. "Oh no, little buddy. Looks like you're on the naughty list this year. Santa left you reindeer poop!" He reached inside and pulled a handful of reindeer shit from the stocking.

Adam screamed and tried to crab walk backward but the

knives kept him pinned to the ground. He pulled and felt the blades tear at his feet but couldn't pull hard enough to free himself.

Sprinkles stalked forward, clutching wet chunks of shit. It ran through his fingers, dripping to the floor. He kicked at the knife closest to him. Waves of agony shot through Adam's foot, lancing up his leg. He screamed and Sprinkles darted forward, ramming a fistful of shit down his throat.

Adam gagged, choking on the shit. He coughed, his body trying to eject the excrement, but Sprinkles jammed another fistful of feces in his mouth.

Adam panicked, the smell and taste of the shit causing him to vomit, but the shit was wedged into the back of his throat and the surge of regurgitation caught around the shit, causing him to choke.

Adam's vision turned black around the edges as he choked on his own vomit and reindeer shit.

"We've got more work to do, little buddy," Sprinkles said, flicking his wrist, invoking Santa's magic. A fine mist of icelike crystals snaked from Sprinkles' fingertips toward Adam. Santa's magic swirled around the boy, making him lighter. With the aid of Santa's magic, Sprinkles dragged him to the recliner in the corner of the room and managed to sit him in the chair.

Sprinkles stripped the lights from the Christmas tree and began decorating.

CHAPTER TWENTY

Cindy twitched violently in her sleep, a noise from upstairs startling her awake. She groaned, rubbing her neck as she sat up. The movie was over. Cindy had fallen asleep shortly after it started. Once she realized the movie was too much for her to watch, rather than admitting it to her brother and sister, she'd placed the television on mute and closed her eyes. Her plan had been a simple one: lie on the couch with her eyes closed, *not* watching the movie until she heard someone coming down the basement steps, then she'd simply hit the **<MUTE>** button again and pretend she'd been watching all along. It never occurred to her that nobody knew she was watching the movie to begin with. She could have simply put something else on, but at twelve, common sense wasn't a common characteristic.

But nobody had come down the steps and she'd stayed on the couch with her eyes closed for so long she eventually dozed off. The armrest was a poor substitute for a pillow.

Where is everyone? They should have come down already.

Worst of all, she'd forgotten to bake the cookies. Someone was upstairs making a bunch of noise. Hopefully, whoever was stomping around like Godzilla had the courtesy to throw the cookies in the oven, especially since she'd laid everything out already. All they had to do was preheat the oven and place the pre-cut dough on the sheets before tossing them in the oven. The moment the thought came and went in Cindy's mind, she knew nobody had done it. They were all a bunch of lazy jerks, no doubt waiting for her to make the cookies. God forbid one of them should make themselves useful tonight.

"All right, I guess I'll get the cookies started and see what the heck everyone is doing," Cindy said, making her way to the basement stairs. She stopped and slipped her feet into the comfy Ugg slippers her father had bought her as an early Christmas present. As her foot hit the first step, Cindy was already thinking about how much of the cookie dough she would eat, rather than bake.

On her wall-mounted television, *Cult of Chucky* played. Katy wasn't sure why she let Jimmy decide on the movie. They'd agreed on watching a movie rather than listening to music. Katy figured whatever was going to happen would happen. She'd promised Jimmy to slow things down, but secretly she hoped he would make *some* kind of move. Over an hour into the movie and he was sitting on the opposite side of the bed, enamored with the events transpiring. For now, she would stick to her promise but next time, she was picking the movie. It was going to be something he hated, so he'd be more apt to talk to her, or something that would get his engine going, so he'd be more apt to at least make out with her.

Looking at the clock on her phone, Katy realized they'd forgotten about movie night with Cindy. The little runt would never let her hear the end of it. She stood up and stretched, ready to break the bad news to Jimmy—Chucky could wait. It was Cindy's turn to pick a movie.

"Did you hear that?" Katy asked.

"Huh?"

She turned the volume down on the soundbar. The thing had been so loud he barely registered her voice a few feet away.

"I don't know. It sounded like someone yelling."

Jimmy shook his head. "I didn't hear anything."

"I definitely heard something."

"It was probably Adam or Bobby playing video games."

Katy and Jimmy both jumped, startled by the sound of the floor-to-ceiling sliding glass door imploding. Glass shrapnel flew through the room, peppering both teens. Katy held her arm over her face, screaming, while Jimmy looked away, shielding his eyes. Small cuts from flying shards appeared on their faces. A small piece of glass stuck in Katy's hand.

Chad Reynolds, adorned in full Santa costume, stepped through the opening he'd smashed in the door, dragging an axe behind him.

Katy screamed again. Jimmy pushed her aside, stepping in between her and the lunatic Santa. He was either unaware of the weapon trailing behind Chad, or playing the hero despite it.

The red and white Santa outfit was soaked in blood. The beard on the man's face was the real deal, no cheap costume, and it, too, was stained red with blood and viscera.

"Ho Ho Ho," Chad said. His grin revealed yellow teeth with black streaks running across them. One incisor was missing, replaced with a small gold nub.

Jimmy stepped forward, cocking his arm back. He launched a wide looping punch, but before the blow made it anywhere near the target, Chad swung his right arm—the one brandishing the axe—forward. The axe slid across the floor alongside Chad before rising in an arc, the blade burying itself in Jimmy's groin, cleaving him from cock to navel before getting stuck.

Jimmy looked down and screamed, a look of shock rather than pain painted across his face.

Chad wrenched the axe down, and a geyser of blood sprayed from the newly formed cleft in Jimmy's groin.

Up to that point, it all happened so quickly that Katy was frozen in place. But when the blood started spurting out of the cleft carved where Jimmy's cock had been, she woke from her trance. Jimmy was done for, she knew. Rather than staying and becoming another victim, she turned and ran from the bedroom, fumbling in her pocket to remove her cell phone. Trails of spittle ran down her chin from screaming. She flew down the stairs and without missing a beat, unlocked her phone.

No service.

"Shit," she said as she turned the corner at the bottom of the stairs. Katy was about to put the phone away when she remembered emergency services could be contacted with no service.

She dialed 911 and put the phone to her ear.

"Nine-one-one, what's your emergency?"

Red and green flashing lights pulled her attention away from the phone. She shrieked, dropping the phone to the carpet.

Adam was tied to the living room recliner with the Christmas tree lights. They flashed alternating colors of red and green; the cords wound tight around his body and in some places, dug into his flesh. The tree topper—a giant gold star—was shoved into his mouth, the top point piercing through the palate, forcing its way into his nasal cavity. The side points ripped through his cheeks and the lower two points impaled their way out either side of his lower jaw. His eyeballs were no longer in their sockets; instead, one was placed in each palm of his hands, which were tied to the recliner palms facing the ceiling. Red glass ball ornaments were shoved into the orbital cavities where his eyes had once been. Adam's entire face was covered in blood, and streaks of brown ran from his lips down the corners of his mouth.

Various ornaments were hooked into his bare chest. There was Jonesy's paw print, all three Feltcher children's painted handprints, Katy's horror movie ornaments, and Mom and Dad's two peas in a pod ornament. Adam had been transformed into the Feltcher family tree.

A tree skirt lay at his feet, the green cloth stained dark with the blood and shit coming from Jonesy's mangled, headless body.

"No, no, no," Katy said. Who was the sick fuck in the Santa costume, and why had he come here tonight? Jimmy was dead, and Adam a grisly tableau of a Christmas tree, but why? She'd never seen that man in her life. Where had this sick fuck come from?

Behind her, Katy heard a scurrying noise. She spun around, expecting to see the maniac blocking her path, axe hoisted over his shoulder and ready to take her head off with one swing.

But the man wasn't there, only Sprinkles, the elf Cindy had been carrying around.

The thing was worse for wear when Cindy had found it in the attic. Cracks littered its frame, rips and stains adorned the green tunic. Some of its dirty blond hair ripped out. But now, Sprinkles had done such a number on Adam that the elf was now soaked with his blood. Pieces of flesh and other unidentifiable organic matter clung to the green hat and tunic.

Above her, Katy heard the thunderous pounding of the crazed man patrolling the upstairs. No doubt it wouldn't be long until he came downstairs to add to his body count. If the sounds of his footsteps were any indication, he was already making his way to the stairs. The monster seemed to be in no rush, and why should he be? The storm raging outside was going to make escape impossible. Survival? Unlikely. Dad wouldn't be home for a while. Maybe if she could get to one of his guns, she'd stand a chance. But that was a big *if*. She'd never learned how to shoot, despite her father begging her to at least learn the basics. Katy had laughed at him. Told her father if it ever came down to her being the last line of self-defense, they were fucked anyway, so what was the point?

She wasn't laughing now.

Katy eyed the elf again. Something seemed off about it. She swore it was in a different position than it had been before she'd gotten lost in her mind thinking about the maniac upstairs. Thinking of Sprinkles brought her mind to Cindy. Jesus Christ, how could she forget her sister? She needed to find her. With any luck, she was in the basement, hiding. She'd witnessed Jimmy being murdered and stumbled across Adam's desecrated corpse. Bobby and Cindy were the only two unaccounted for and if they weren't in the basement, Katy had to assume they were dead, probably strung up somewhere on the property in another grotesque display.

Santa's footsteps grew closer now, hitting the top step.

"Shit," Katy said. She took off running like a bat out of hell.

As she ran past, Sprinkles' grey eyes shot open, his head following her as she made her mad dash to the basement. He popped up and darted toward the front porch, the bell on his hat jingling with each step.

CHAPTER TWENTY-ONE

Jack Feltcher made his way home through the snow. The accumulation wasn't a problem for him. A few years ago, even before Courtney had died and he began crushing overtime, he'd purchased a plow package for his winter truck. The truck got little use—it was a gas guzzler—but any time there was a significant amount of snowfall, he drove it to work. With the prison being a twenty-four seven operation, a small, front-wheel drive vehicle made little sense for his winter work commute. A decent set of snow tires and all-wheel drive did wonders, although he did still have to be careful over icy roads.

What *was* a problem for Jack's commute was the damn wind gusts of sixty miles per hour battering his vehicle and destroying visibility. Cranking back and forth as fast as the arms would move, his windshield wipers were getting one hell of a workout. Even so, it wasn't nearly enough. He was stuck driving far slower than he should have been able to with the truck. Already tired from a long week of work, the sloth-like speed he was currently traveling at was getting on his last nerve.

Jack tried to control his breathing, calm himself down. He

needed to remember he was headed home for the holiday. Home to his kids. Plenty of his coworkers didn't receive that luxury this year, so he knew he should be thankful.

In his truck, the police radio scanner—something he'd always loved listening to, a habit he'd gotten from his grandfather and tried to share with Adam to no avail—cut through the drone of the heating ducts.

Dispatch to unit three.

This is unit three, go ahead, dispatch.

Unit three, if you're still in the area we've got an emergency call from Dale Avenue. Triangulation puts it at number One Dale Avenue. I received a nine-one-one call with no response other than a woman screaming and incoherent mumbling. The line cut out and I haven't been able to reach the caller back.

Roger that, dispatch. I'm about thirty minutes out with the weather, twenty-five if I'm flying. I'm still the closest unit; one and two are both responding to vehicle accidents on the other side of town. Headed that way now, over and out.

"One Dale Avenue," Jack said. "You've gotta be fucking kidding me, that's my house! Why wouldn't they call me?" Jack pulled his phone out of the center console, tapped the screen.

No reception. The storm must have given the tower a beating, leaving only emergency lines open.

Jack gripped the steering wheel and pressed harder on the accelerator, taking the truck far past a speed at which he could safely drive under the current conditions.

CHAPTER TWENTY-TWO

As she was making her way up the basement stairs, Cindy heard Katy scream. She flew up the steps to see what was wrong with her sister. Turning the corner, she and Katy collided in the rear hallway, Cindy falling backward on her ass while Katy merely stopped in place.

"Holy shit, you're okay, thank God," Katy said.

"What do you mean I'm okay? Where is everyone?"

"They're . . ." she stopped for a moment, trailing off before ignoring the question. "Is Bobby with you?" asked Katy.

"No, I thought he was with Adam. I figured you guys left me down there because you both had your friends and didn't want to hang out with me.

Katy extended her hands out and helped Cindy up. She stood and was rewarded for the action with a bear hug that threatened to suffocate her. "Get off of me," Cindy said.

"Sorry. Look, we've gotta go. Something bad is going on. We have to get out of here."

"What do you mean 'something bad is going on'? Katy, you're scaring me. Where is everyone?"

"They're fucking dead, Cindy. I didn't want to say it, but if you don't stop asking so many questions and start running, we are too. Now get to my damn car!"

Cindy had no choice but to hurry behind her sister as she ran outside, onto the back porch. In the rush, Cindy didn't have time to put her shoes on and the cold, wet snow immediately bit through her socks. "Stop," Cindy said, "I've gotta put my shoes on!"

"We don't have time for that. The car will be warm once we get the heat going. If we don't get in that damn car, it won't matter how fucking cold your feet are. Someone is in the house and everyone is dead. What don't you understand about that?"

Whether Cindy didn't believe Katy the first time she'd said it, or the gravity of the situation hadn't yet hit her twelve-year-old mind, hearing it a second time hammered the point home. Cindy closed her mouth and moved her legs as fast as they'd take her, following her sister through the cold and hopefully to safety.

"Oh Jesus, fuck!" Katy said. "Don't look over there."

At first, Cindy had no idea what Katy was talking about, but you can't tell a twelve-year-old that and expect them *not* to look.

Cindy regretted letting her curiosity get the best of her. Off to the side of the deck, she saw Bobby's discarded corpse in the crimson-stained snow. Cindy couldn't see much of the body because of the surrounding snowfall—and didn't want to—but she could see he'd lost a lot of blood, and after what she'd discovered near the sledding hills, this second dead body made her heart race. She was sweating despite the cold weather and her breath came in quick, hitching gasps even though they'd only started to run a few moments ago.

They were off the deck in a few strides, Bobby's corpse behind them but still clear in her mind.

The snow was five or six inches deep, at least. Cindy couldn't tell, but she knew it was difficult to pump her legs through the heavy accumulation and they burned from exhaustion.

"Katy, I can't breathe, and my legs burn. I have to stop," she said between quick, shallow breaths. "Why am I sweating? It's freezing."

"You're having a panic attack, Cindy. Try to control your breathing. I know it's hard, but focus on slow, steady breaths in, and slow, steady breaths out. We haven't run that far for you to be tired or out of breath yet. We've only turned the corner. Look, the cars are right there. Keep going!"

Cindy trusted her sister, but it was tough to take that advice when your chest felt like someone bear-hugging you and your legs felt like there were bowling balls attached to your feet. She tried to control her breathing like Katy had told her, and it helped a little, but she still felt like she was fading fast.

After what seemed like forever but was really less than a minute, the girls made it to Katy's car. Cindy stood by the passenger door, pulling the handle, but it was locked. Katy hit the button on her key fob twice; the car doors unlocked with two beeps.

They hopped into the vehicle, Katy pushed the **<START>** button, and Cindy buckled her seat belt. Katy pressed the button for **<REVERSE>** and stomped on the gas.

The car didn't budge. The tires didn't even seem to spin in the snow. Katy took her foot off the gas, waited a moment for the engine to stop revving before trying again.

Again, nothing.

"Shit!" Katy punched the steering wheel and opened the car door. Cindy screamed as her sister exited the vehicle, "Don't leave me in here!"

"I'm not leaving you. I've gotta see what's wrong."

Cindy sat in the passenger seat, the feeling of smothering heavy on her chest again. Her skin felt prickly and hot, and each breath she took felt like the oxygen was going anywhere *but* her lungs. She knew Katy didn't leave her, but not being able to see her sister made everything more terrifying.

"They're flat," Katy yelled from outside. Cindy barely heard her over the wind.

The rear driver's side window shattered, glass flew inside the vehicle. Katy's face had hit the window and destroyed it. Cindy screamed. Some lunatic she'd never seen before, dressed in a Santa costume, gripped her sister's head by the ponytail.

Cindy howled like a banshee.

Katy's nose was crushed, blood pouring from the pancaked mass of cartilage. Strips of flesh hung from her cheeks. Speckles of glass pocked her skin. Her mouth hung slack, lips split, a few teeth missing.

The man in the red suit yanked her backward by the ponytail, tossing her to the ground.

Cindy didn't know what to do. There was nowhere to go. She couldn't drive a car, but even if she could, it wouldn't go anywhere. Katy had already tried.

She had to run for help. There was no other choice. If she could get to Ms. Kettle's house maybe she could call the police.

Cindy fumbled with the buckle, but the crippling fear made it difficult to perform a routine task such as undoing a seat belt.

Too late, Santa was at her door. He swung it open and wrapped his arm around her little neck, squeezing against the carotid artery until she passed out.

Chad Reynolds, with his suit soaked in blood, entrails, sweat, and snow, tossed Cindy over his shoulder. He walked around to the opposite side of the vehicle and grabbed Katy by the ankle, dragging her back toward their house.

"Can't wait for your daddy to get home, girls," Chad said before bursting out a seasonal "Ho Ho Ho."

He'd finally done it. For the Feltcher family, Christmas was canceled.

From the darkness, Sprinkles watched the Santa imper-sonator carry his playthings back to the house.

CHAPTER TWENTY-THREE

Cindy's eyes fluttered open, tears blurring her vision. She blinked them away, and bit by bit, her sight returned, banishing the encroaching blackness. The relentless pounding in her head and the constant ache in her neck made it hard for her to focus on anything else. She flexed her toes, the uncomfortable sensation of pins and needles coaxing forth the memory of running through the snow. Of Katy being assaulted. Of Santa Claus hurting her.

Trying to stand, Cindy found the task impossible. Her legs wouldn't budge. Her arms, too, wouldn't respond. Looking down, she saw Christmas garland binding her limbs to a dining room chair. Next to her, also tied to a chair, was Katy.

Cindy tried to scream, but something was lodged in her mouth, tied around the back of her head, preventing her from calling out. The sound died in her throat.

Chad had brought two dining room chairs to the living room and set them up a few feet apart, strapping the girls in next to their dead brother.

It took a few minutes after Cindy regained consciousness before she saw Adam's corpse. When she did, something inside of her broke. Whatever part of her that had kept a glimmer of hope that they'd live to see another day, gave up. And she screamed her muffled screams until her throat was raw. She sobbed, choking on tears. Cindy knew what was in store for both she and Katy.

Chad entered the living room. "I thought I heard a commotion in here. What's wrong, little girl? Are you afraid of Santa Claus?"

Cindy's eyes bugged out of her head. In his hand, Chad held a large black handgun—her father's gun. She didn't know what kind it was or any sort of details, but she had seen the gun on a few occasions when he'd been cleaning it and recognized it instantly. He never kept it in a safe or locked up. When Cindy had asked her father why it was so easily within reach, he'd simply replied, "What good is a self-defense tool if you're dead before you can get to it?"

It made sense to her in the way that kids simply accept what their parents tell them as fact. And growing up with a father who worked in law enforcement, she'd always understood that when proper precautions were taken, guns were safe. But when they were mishandled, they were deadly. The Feltcher children never played with the weapon because to them, it wasn't some unknown mystery. It didn't have the allure of some forbidden thing, locked up and never to be spoken of.

But now? Now Cindy saw the gun for what it was: an instrument of death. No matter how you sliced it, defense or not, a gun's purpose was to kill. She wished her father hadn't been so nonchalant about the weapon. An inanimate object she'd once thought of with indifference now looked cold. Lifeless. It frightened her to the core.

Chad paced back and forth in front of the girls before suddenly stopping, leaning toward Cindy, and pressing the gun against the soft spot under her chin. "You *should* be afraid, little girl. I'm not Santa. There's no such thing as Santa.

Christmas miracles aren't real. But Christmas nightmares? You're looking at one."

Muffled screams pulled Chad's attention from Cindy. He turned toward the eldest Feltcher sibling. "Ahhh, you're awake," Chad said, pressing the gun against Katy's leg, sliding the steel barrel of the weapon up her thigh, and resting it against her groin. He pressed the weapon against her. Katy's muffled screams grew louder, but they were still useless. Nobody was coming to save them. Cindy didn't know why this man was hurting them, but she knew it didn't matter. Her dad taught her all about men like the crazed lunatic before her. Some men were just bad, and there was no fixing them, no reasoning with them. They belonged behind bars, the key tossed away like the lives they'd snuffed out.

Here was one such monster. In her home.

Katy struggled with her restraints, but unlike Cindy, Chad had used rope to restrain Katy. He must have known garland wouldn't hold an eighteen-year-old. She rocked back and forth, threatening to tip the chair. Without warning, Chad pulled the gun from Katy's crotch and pistol-whipped her across the face, smashing the cold steel against her jaw. Blood streamed around the gag. She swallowed a dislodged tooth.

"You might wonder why I'm doing this. I know I would if I were sitting in your chairs. The reason is simple. I'm not a lunatic. This isn't some random home invasion. I'm here for one reason. Your father took five years of my life from me. Once that happened, I lost my spot in the group home that I'd applied to and I lost the job I had lined up for when I *should* have been released. Years later, when I *did* get released, I had nowhere to go. Nothing to look forward to. I didn't have anyone to help me or guide me. I spent all that fucking time in prison while this world was changing. And they let me out with no fucking resources, nothing to help make sure I wouldn't come back. So I said fuck it. I've killed someone before. It would be nothing to do it again. Then I can go right back to Glenwood Correctional Institute, eat my three meals a day, and have a warm roof over my head. I live better in prison than I do as a free man. Gotta love America, right?"

Cindy cried hysterically. She didn't know what the hell this man was talking about. All she pulled from his long-winded speech was the fact that he was going to kill them because of some grudge he had against her father. The man who was never around anymore was somehow responsible for her impending death, and as usual, he wasn't around to save her.

"But when I got here, I was pleasantly surprised to see this fucker in the chair over here. One of you is a sick fuck. Who could do that to their brother? I don't think it was the little one," Chad said, pointing the gun at Cindy. "She's much too small to have done this. I think it was you."

As he finished the sentence, he swung the gun toward Katy, but before the gun pointed at her, Sprinkles hopped from the top of the Christmas tree, holding a stocking out. He pulled the red and white mantle decoration over Chad's head as he fell, blinding him and throwing off his aim. An explosion rang Cindy's bell as the gun fired into the ceiling. Plaster dust fell to the floor like the snow outside, dotting Cindy's face, making her sneeze.

As Sprinkles hit the floor, he tucked his knees and rolled behind Chad, stabbing him in the calf with his sharpened candy cane. Chad swiped down at Sprinkles, attempting to smack the hellish elf, finding nothing but space—the elf was much too quick. Sprinkles ran laps around Chad, slashing and poking with the candy cane, blood splattering the living room with each strike.

Chad ripped the stocking from his head. When at last he saw the Christmas toy come to life attacking him, he screamed and kicked out with his bloodied leg, hitting Sprinkles in the chest. The elf flew backward, smacking the brick surrounding the fireplace with a hard *thwack*. He plopped to the floor and lay still.

"What the fuck is that thing?" Chad pointed the gun at Sprinkles and fired, but Sprinkles rolled to the side, narrowly avoiding the projectile. He popped up and ran at Chad, taking the psychopath by surprise once more. Chad fired two more quick shots in defense, but they struck the ground, missing the intended target.

"You're not Santa, you're just a fat fuck in a red suit!" Sprinkles yelled as he flicked his wrist. A second candy cane weapon appeared courtesy of the real Santa's corrupted Christmas magic. Sprinkles leaped at Chad, digging a candy cane into each of Chad's thighs.

Wide-eyed, Cindy watched as the unimaginable events unfolded. The elf moved so quickly he was little more than a blur.

Sprinkles alternated pulling each candy cane out and stabbing higher, using them like ice climber axes, ascending the body of the lunatic in the Santa outfit. Chad screamed, tried to retaliate but his weak swipes with the gun weren't enough to knock the toy loose, and Chad was too scared to pull the trigger, afraid he'd hit himself.

Blood leaked from each puncture wound inflicted by the candy canes, which now ran from Chad's thighs all the way to his upper chest.

Grasping the candy canes, Sprinkles pulled himself up and clamped his razor-sharp teeth on Chad's lips, pulled his head away, and spat Chad's lips to the floor.

Chad screamed, falling to his knees. Sprinkles pulled the candy canes from Chad's chest and stabbed again and again until the Santa imposter sunk to the floor, lying in a spreading pool of blood.

With a snap of elfin fingers, the candy canes were gone.

"My, he was on the naughty list, all right. You should see what he did to the lady across the street," said Sprinkles.

Both girls cried in their chairs, helpless to move. Their lives were at the mercy of a deranged Christmas toy come to life.

Sprinkles retrieved the gun Chad had dropped and flipped it over in his hands, inspecting the firearm. Without warning, the gun went off. Fired indoors, the report of the pistol was deafening. Cindy's ears rang as if someone had boxed them. Next to her, a .40 caliber round blasted through Katy's left eye and punched out through the back of her skull. From the exit wound, an explosion of blood and flecks of skull and brain matter painted the bay window and Christmas tree with gore.

"Oh, Sprinkles is a naughty little elf! You'll have to forgive me, they didn't teach us weapons training at the North Pole! I thought it was a cap gun!" Sprinkles said, tossing the gun aside.

Cindy's bladder let go. A stream of warm piss ran down her leg as she continued to struggle against the garland restraint. Snot and tears soaked her face, the neck of her pink nighty stained dark.

"Is that piss? Sprinkles *loves* piss," the elf said as he ran his hard, plastic hand across her ankle. He brought a finger to his lip and licked it. "Tastes like fear."

Sprinkles hopped on Cindy's lap and flicked his wrist, using Santa's magic to conjure a pair of rusty pliers. He leaned forward, whispering in Cindy's ear, "Did you know I always wanted to be a dentist? I've been studying, it's fascinating, you have no idea! Molars and bicuspids and incisors!"

The makeshift gag Chad had used to dampen Cindy's cries left plenty of room to work with the front teeth. Slowly, he brought the tool to Cindy's mouth. Cindy felt it clamp down on one of her canines. She screamed as loud as the gag would allow, rocking, powerless to fight back. The pliers wiggled, and at first she only felt a slight pressure, but soon the constant back-and-forth movement increased in intensity and the pressure turned to pain.

Sprinkles tugged harder, using his feet for leverage.

A shooting pain ripped through her mouth, followed by a slow, wet, tearing noise as the tooth ripped from its socket.

Sprinkles held the tooth up as if it were a prized trophy.

Cindy was spared the sight; she'd passed out from the pain.

Sprinkles continued the task at hand while Cindy remained unconscious, the only respite she'd get from the sadistic dentistry.

CHAPTER TWENTY-FOUR

Jack Feltcher turned onto Dale Avenue. The drive had been a harrowing affair. He'd had a few close calls and had even caused someone else's vehicle to careen off the road into a snowbank. He hoped like hell that the occupants of the vehicle were okay, but he needed to get home to his kids. There had been no radio chatter about the patrol car arriving on the scene, and the absence of flashing lights told Feltcher he made it home before the responding police cruiser.

He took his foot off the accelerator, eased the brakes. He made it this far without crashing. It wouldn't do to hit a tree or utility pole this late in the game. Luckily, they lived in the first house, which coincidently was one of only two houses even visible from the beginning of the street. The next closest neighbor was a half mile farther down.

Jack pulled up to the front of the house and noticed a few things. First, the lights at the Kettle residence were on and her front door was wide open. Sandra Kettle had a lot of visitors at her house at all times of the day and night, and while they lived in a quiet, secluded area, it wasn't like Sandra or her visitors to leave the door open. The neighborhood was safe, but not *that* safe. No place was so welcoming in 2023.

Neighborhood safety statistics aside, she wouldn't leave her door wide open during a nor'easter. The open door was ominous. A warning sign of what was to come.

The second thing Jack noticed was that both cars in the driveway seemed to sit low to the ground, as if they were both on flats.

"Jesus Christ," Jack said, swinging the car door open. He ran through the snow to his front door, not bothering to inspect the vehicles. There was no time. First, he needed to make sure his children were safe, property damage could wait. He drew his sidearm—an M&P 40 Shield—from his belt holster while running through the snow.

In his home, he kept a GLOCK 23 for defense and hoped that either Adam or Katy grabbed it and had retained enough of what he'd told them about it to keep themselves safe.

But what Jack's heart hoped for and what his brain knew to be true were two different things. None of the children showed any interest in learning how to use firearms for self-defense. They'd often make fun of him for trying to teach them.

Jack ran up the steps and as he entered the front door, from the corner of his eye, he saw some sort of red spatter on the bay window. He pushed the image out of his head, tried to remain levelheaded until he'd assessed the scene.

The moment he stepped in the front hallway, his heart dropped. He saw blood on the carpet runner and what looked to be Jonesy's body in the entryway to the living room. Jack kept his firearm at the ready as he crept forward, scanning for signs of his children or anyone else who might be hiding.

When he reached the headless cat, Jack's eyes taking in the carnage of the living room, they settled on something his brain couldn't comprehend as real. All three of his children restrained on chairs. Adam and Katy appeared to be dead, Adam clearly tortured. Both girls' backs were facing Jack, but the hole in Katy's skull told him everything he needed to know.

Perched atop his twelve-year-old baby girl was the hideous elf toy his wife had loved. From his vantage point, he could only see a portion of it, but every inch of the monstrosity he *could* see was covered in blood and viscera. Sprinkles the elf wriggled back and forth. Whatever he was doing, he grunted as if exerting great force.

Jack couldn't believe that was a thought he'd actually just had.

"What the fuck?" Jack lifted the gun, training it on the elf. There was no room for error. If his shot was off the mark, there would be a bullet hole in Cindy's head that matched the one in Katy's. He timed his breath with the elf's back-and-forth movements. At last, Sprinkles stopped and held up a pair of pliers, a tooth held within their grasp.

Jack took the shot.

Sprinkles flew backward, a cloud of plastic shards exploding in the air as Sprinkles fell to the ground. The elf rolled a few feet and came to a stop next to a bloody and battered Santa Claus. "What the fuck is going on?" Jack asked as he ran to his daughter.

It took a moment, but as Jack approached, he recognized the man in the Santa costume. Chad Reynolds. What the hell was Chad Reynolds doing in his home? None of this made any sense. Who had killed him? The elf? The thought was absurd, and Jack knew it, but had he not just witnessed the elf ripping his daughter's teeth out?

He pulled the makeshift gag from her mouth, wincing at the sight of her mangled face. The thing had ripped out all of the top and bottom teeth from the canines inward. Jack ripped at the garland restraint. He was laser focused on rescuing his last living family member. First, he'd lost his wife. Now, his two oldest children. He couldn't lose his baby too.

In the chair, Cindy's chest rose and fell with slow, shallow breaths. Still alive, thank God. Jack needed to get her an ambulance. He'd take her to the truck and call on the police band.

Chad came to, beaten and bloodied. He opened his eyes to see his nemesis, Jack Feltcher, rescuing his daughter. No way was that son of a bitch besting him. If Chad was going to Hell, he'd take Jack along for the ride.

Vision hazy with blood, Chad felt around, looking for something, anything he could use to take the fucker out. He rose slowly to his knees and from the corner of his eye, saw the metal handle of the poker sticking out from the fireplace.

He yanked it free, scattering burning logs onto the floor. The carpet caught fire behind him.

Alerted by the noise, Jack Feltcher turned around and locked eyes with Chad. The look of surprise on his face was the best thing Chad had ever seen.

With the last bit of strength he could muster, Chad shot his arm forward, punching through Jack's chest with the red-hot poker, piercing his heart. The searing poker exited through Jack's back.

Jack looked down and grabbed for the poker but was dead before he knew what happened. He dropped to the ground.

Chad fell beside his nemesis, staring into his lifeless eyes as he waited for the reaper to take him.

Officer Jay Durgin pulled up to the house on Dale Avenue. There was a truck, still running, abandoned in the driveway. Officer Durgin exited his Ford Explorer and surveyed the scene. It took only a moment for him to see the warm glow of flames through the large bay window at the front of the house.

Durgin took off through the snow as fast as his legs would carry him. He entered through the front door and saw a bloodbath, along with a roaring fire that quickly grew.

The living room was a fucking massacre: five bodies, all appeared to be dead. Durgin keyed the radio clipped to his jacket. "Dispatch, I'm gonna need fire and rescue at number One Dale Avenue. It's a damn slaughterhouse in here."

To his left, he heard a cough. It was the little girl. She was alive! He lifted her up gently, not knowing the extent of her injuries. "I'm here, honey. I'm gonna get you out of here," he said.

The girl's face was a train wreck. Blood oozed from her mouth, a gaping black hole. What happened to her teeth? Durgin couldn't tell for sure, but there were quite a few missing. Cindy coughed, spitting blood on Officer Durgin's face. His heart wept for her. He needed to get this little girl to safety. He had to keep his eyes open. He'd run into the residence knowing nothing of what to expect, and what he'd found in the living room told him danger could lurk around any corner. The person who did this could be one of the corpses strewn about the living room.

Or they could be on the loose.

Carrying Cindy, Durgin took a step toward the front door. Cindy sobbed and spoke a garbled mess of vocalizations he couldn't understand—the damage to her mouth too great. She pointed at something behind him.

Durgin turned around, looking for any sign of what she was trying to show him.

A large Christmas elf doll among the dead bodies.

She wants the doll. After whatever she's been through tonight, the least I can do is save the elf. This might be the only possession saved from the fire.

Officer Durgin turned around and snatched the elf. The thing was disgusting. He was going to have to clean it off for sure. There were human remains all over it—blood, organic tissue, you name it. The thing should be logged as evidence in whatever case this turns out to be, but Durgin felt so bad for this child whose life was clearly just turned upside down that he couldn't possibly turn her toy in as evidence. As a victim of a house fire as a child, Durgin knew what it was like to lose everything to the hungry flames.

He tucked the elf under his elbow, the only way he could carry it while carrying Cindy out of the burning house. Durgin coughed, the smoke growing thicker. It was time to get out of here, get this little girl to his squad car. The ambulance would be here shortly. He debated bringing her to the emergency room himself since the ambulance hadn't arrived yet, but after taking a look at her, she needed to be checked out by a medical professional. Hopefully, they wouldn't be long.

Durgin ran outside, carrying both the crying child and her elf. She screamed in his arms and spit out an unintelligible garble. Between the hysterics and the damage done to her mouth, there was no way Durgin could understand whatever it was she was trying to tell him.

He let the elf fall to the snow beside the car so he could readjust and open the back door of the cruiser. Durgin placed Cindy on the seat, letting her sprawl out in the back. He noticed her socks were drenched, so he pulled them off. Not knowing the details of how everything went down, Durgin had no clue how long her feet had been exposed to the wet socks, but removing them and blasting the heat in the cruiser would be the quickest way to warm them up.

Durgin closed the door and grabbed the elf. He'd clean it

off as best he could before giving it to the child. That way she wouldn't have to look at the gore coating the entirety of it. He walked to the driver's side door and hopped in, placing the elf on the passenger seat.

Dispatch came over the radio. Emergency services were two minutes away.

Cindy Feltcher sobbed in the back seat, her life forever changed. Everyone in her family was dead.

Durgin looked at her in the rearview mirror. *For her, Christmas is canceled forever.*

EPILOGUE

Officer Durgin had spent most of the night typing an incident report for his supervisor. All the bodies discovered in the house were presumed to belong to the Feltcher family except for two. A third body, not of the Feltcher clan, was discovered on the rear deck. At some point, they'd need little Cindy Feltcher to identify the bodies if no other family members could be tracked down to handle the grim task.

Unfortunate, but necessary.

Jack's supervisor had spoken with detectives and described the members of the household based on a photograph on Jack's desk. And while there were three bodies discovered not belonging to the immediate family, it didn't mean there was no relation. It was Christmas Eve, and not unreasonable to think other distant family members had been present that evening.

In due time, DNA evidence would reveal that information.

Once EMS had arrived, they loaded the Feltcher child in the back of the ambulance and began to stabilize her as they drove to the ER, leaving Durgin to work the scene with fellow responding officers and the fire department. Shortly after

EMS left, Durgin had walked across the street to interview potential witnesses. But when he realized the front door had been open since the moment he'd first arrived at the Feltcher residence, he knew something was wrong.

Though Durgin had suspected foul play, he hadn't expected to walk in on what appeared to be a brutal rape and murder. Between the two crime scene reports, Durgin had stayed hours after his shift was over, making sure his first responder report was accurate. Otherwise, the chance of solving the crimes would be severely diminished.

Durgin emerged from the officers' locker room, freshly showered and changed out of his uniform. He'd snuck the elf into the station in his duffel bag and before beginning his desk work, he tossed its clothing in the washing machine and dryer. By the time Durgin had finished his reports, the elf's clothes were clean. He'd been surprised when he removed the tunic and hat from the dryer; they looked almost pristine. The blood and stains were faded, barely visible.

Looking at the shirt again, Durgin swore he'd seen a bullet hole in the damn thing, but clearly, he had been mistaken. The result of sleep deprivation and high stress.

Leaving the station, Durgin tossed the elf in his car before hopping into the driver's seat and taking off for the night.

He had one more stop before heading home. *It would be a pleasant surprise*, he thought, *if I bring the Feltcher girl her elf. It was, after all, the only possession she had left.*

Durgin pulled out of the parking lot and drove a few minutes down the road before turning onto the highway on-ramp. The snow was still coming down, but the town's snow removal trucks had done a nice job clearing much of the main roads, and the state had done an excellent job with the highway. Driving a Toyota 4Runner also helped Durgin's ability to commute in poor weather conditions.

Snap.

Durgin looked to the passenger seat. He'd heard a noise,

like someone snapping their fingers. At first, he thought maybe he'd taken the ramp a bit hard and the elf had knocked against the door, but the doll remained sitting in the very same position Durgin had placed him.

I really need to hit the hay, I'm hearing shit now. I'll just bring this thing to one of the nurses. Tomorrow I'll check on the girl before I head into work.

Snap.

Durgin looked again, confident he wasn't hearing things.

Sprinkles' eyes shot open, and he lunged across the seat. "Merry Christmas, Piggy!"

Durgin screamed.

When the sharp tip of the candy cane pierced his eyeball, he jerked the wheel. The last thing Durgin heard was Sprinkles' maniacal cackle and the loud horn of an eighteen-wheeler before it hit his 4Runner head-on.

BONUS STORY

Want to know more about how the Santa from the prologue came to inherit the title and magic? Read this bonus short story!

THE TREE FARM

Corporal Justin Pitts took a knee on the cold, hard ground. Lost in a maze of pine trees deep within Big John's tree farm, Corporal Pitts needed a battle plan. First things first, he had to stop the bleeding. One of those little freaks stabbed him with a candy cane. Why the fuck was that thing so sharp, anyway? Come to think of it, there were a few questions Pitts had in mind. Questions such as *what the fuck are those things?* And *why the fuck were they trying to kill me?*

Corporal Pitts pondered these questions, and more, all while taking in the overpowering aroma of the holiday season. Tree sap and pine needles assaulted his nostrils. He loved the smell, loved the season. This should have been a dream come true. When he responded to a Craigslist advertisement seeking one Marine for a Toys for Tots collection campaign, he never considered the dream might be a nightmare in disguise. A bit more thought on his part would have led him to question why a campaign the Marine Corps took part in yearly was recruiting on Craigslist, but Pitts had never been much of a deep thinker. If he had been, he might have enlisted in a branch of service that taught you more than how to kill, or at least a different job within the Marine Corps. Still, his love of the holiday season, and his good hearted nature may very well have led him here regardless of branch of service.

Pitts unclasped the gold buckle from his white belt, a staple of the Marine Dress Blue uniform, which was widely considered the finest looking United States military dress uniform. A beauty to gaze upon, Dress Blues were a fucking nightmare to wear. Hell, it was a two man job just to button the damn collar on the thing, but Pitts didn't care about that right now, he was simply happy to have the belt. It would serve well as a tourniquet to stop the bleeding from his thigh. He felt a little woozy and was worried about the amount of blood he'd left in the snow.

Pitts had been helping Santa pack up the display when one of the "elves"... mutated or something. Pitts didn't know, and he didn't care either. The *what* was irrelevant. All he knew for sure was that one moment the thing looked human, the next its face was a scarred, burned mess. Razor teeth protruded from its mouth. Fingernails like talons grew in an instant. The creature ran at him, holding a giant, sharpened candy cane—not that it needed the candy cane with the horrific claws it possessed—and screaming like a banshee. Pitts had never heard a sound like that in his life. A guttural, panic inducing sound. Now, they kept screaming at him from somewhere in the trees. They, because with Pitt's luck, of course there would be more than one of those things. Were they toying with him? The pun, unintended as it was, made Pitts laugh. It was laugh or go nuts. Maybe he *already* had gone mad. Because that made more sense than being chased through a tree farm by murderous, mutant elves. It was certainly plausible that he'd lost his marbles. Back in Afghanistan, all of the Marines had been forced to take Mefloquine once a week to prevent malaria. His squad had lovingly called it malaria Monday. Everyone knew Mefloquine caused crazy ass dreams, but what medical had never told anyone was that in rare cases psychosis had been reported as a side effect. He should have chanced the malaria.

Pitts had to stop himself from going down that rabbit hole. Whether or not he was going mad, all that mattered was getting out of this damn tree farm. If he could do that, he would have plenty of time for a psychological deep dive. Only one man could get him off this fucking farm: Santa.

He had hitched a ride here with Kris Kringle himself, and taking in the scenery from the passenger seat, the size of the farm had impressed Corporal Pitts. He had never seen so many Christmas trees in one place. He hadn't seen a map of the farm, but from what he gathered on the drive in, and the walk to Santa's workshop, Pitts figured he was somewhere in the middle of the farm. He could try to run in one direction, sure. But with the sheer amount of trees on the farm, and known points of reference, it would be easy to get turned around. And who knew what lie on the outer edges of the farm. No, without Santa's guidance, he may never escape the farm.

After Pitts fended off the deranged elf, Santa was nowhere to be found. It was as if he vanished, and in his place, half a dozen of the abominations had appeared. Each one of the creatures equally as deranged and blood-thirsty as his assailant. Wounded, Pitts had taken off like a bat out of hell. He didn't care for his odds of fending off seven knee-high mutants while he was bleeding like a stuck pig.

Pitts removed his dress coat and tossed it in the snow. The jacket restricted far too much, and while he had nothing but a white t-shirt under the jacket, and it was freezing outside, he'd much rather have freedom of movement. He needed to be ready for anything. Pitts rubbed his arms, using the friction to warm himself. If the elves didn't kill him, the cold surely would.

Wanting to test his mobility with the tourniquet, Pitts took a few small steps forward, putting varying amounts of pressure and body weight on the leg to make sure it would hold up. It hurt like a bitch, but it would have to do. His life depended on it.

Hehehehehehehe

Giggling in the trees. Pitts thought it sounded closer than the screeches from earlier. He turned around, peering into the trees for the source of laughter. The falling snow obscured anything further than a few feet in front of him, and the dense rows of pine trees only further blocked his line of sight.

He heard a rustling behind him and turned around in time to see tree branches parting, giving way for a psychotic abomination dressed in classic green and red attire. It rushed straight at Pitts, its tiny legs pistoning, propelling its grotesque body faster than Pitts would have thought possible. Quick as lighting, it closed the distance and swung a severed reindeer antler. Pitts hopped back, narrowly avoiding the antler. A sharp pain shot through his leg. It buckled and he fell flat on his ass, a plume of snow puffing up in the air around him.

Pitts crawled backward as the elf stalked forward. It giggled and stabbed at the air while inching closer to Pitts, a murderous, maniacal expression smeared on its face.

"Don't you think Santa gives us the best toys, Justin?" the elf asked. Its voice pierced Pitts's ears, like nails dragging across a chalkboard.

"What the fuck are you?" asked Pitts.

"I'm an elf, silly! What are you, a dummy?"

Pitts scrambled to his feet. "This is fucking crazy. Why are you doing this?"

"You Marines are naughty boys. And you, Justin, you're on the top of the list. You thought you had gotten away with those things you did. You and your friends did very bad things. *Naughty* things, and Santa said coal wouldn't be enough to fix you." The elf giggled again and leapt through the air.

The elf collided with Pitts hard enough to knock the wind out of him. He fell into the snow once more, tumbling backward, grappling with the elf. That son-of-a-bitch was strong as an ox, and Pitts struggled to gain the upper hand. After some time rolling around in the snow, Pitts managed to mount the elf.

From below, the elf took another swipe at Pitts. This time the antler found its mark. Pitts shirt tore, as did the skin beneath it. A huge gash from pectoral to pectoral appeared, and Pitts wished he had left the jacket on. Any layer of protection would have been better than a plain white T-shirt. Blood splashed across the elf's face, painting its hideous features crimson. It flicked out a long, pointed tongue, running the muscle across its lips and teeth, savoring each drop.

Despite the immense, burning pain from the deep wound, Pitts maintained his position atop the beast. He watched as the monstrosity held its mouth open, trying to catch every drop of blood.

"What a treat, it tastes so sweet!" it rhymed, its gleeful jests made more horrible by its murderous actions.

Cocking his arm, Pitts hit the elf with a haymaker that would have made Mike Tyson proud, but the blow didn't seem to faze the elf; it kicked its legs gleefully and continued to giggle.

"Do it again, you naughty Marine. It's always violence, violence, violence with you naughty jarheads."

Pitts obliged and continued to rain blow after blow upon the elf, shattering its teeth and rearranging its nose. He pounded the elf's face into a bloody pulp, feeling the creature's skeletal structure rearrange from the force of each blow. Pitts didn't relent until his arms were so fatigued he couldn't throw another punch.

When the first punch hadn't so much as phased the elf, Pitts started to worry, but by the time the 21st found its mark, the elf was well and truly fucked.

"Unnggghhh," muttered the elf. It coughed, spraying blood in Pitts' face.

"Just die already, you son-of-a-bitch!" Pitts yelled.

The creature removed the bell from the tip of its hat, and with its last ounce of strength, jingled it. "Santa," it said, "I found that naughty boy. Please don't be mad at me."

The elf lay broken, the snow around it soaked in blood and bits of bone and flesh. The elf's holiday attire was now completely saturated, not only from the snow, but from a massive loss of blood. It had also pissed and shit itself when it expired. Not quite the festive garb it had once been.

Pitts rolled off of the creature and got back to his feet. He had to get out of here, and if what the creature said was the truth, Santa was in on...whatever this was, effectively killing the only plan for survival Pitts had come up with.

Was this some kind of trap to punish him? At least that's what the elf said. Corporal Justin Pitts had a few skeletons in his closet. Many of them gained overseas. How could this *thing* know about any of that?

"Hohoho," a voice bellowed. It was close. "Rudolph, won't you guide my sleigh to that murdering piece of shit?"

"You've gotta be kidding me," said Pitts. He took off, sprinting through the pine trees, not waiting to see what yuletide horrors Santa had in store for him.

Branches whipped Pitts in the face, opening lacerations across his face. Pitts held his hand in front of his face. The last thing he needed was a tree branch impaling an eyeball. He was exhausted, and in great physical pain, bleeding from his chest and the candy cane wound. But he wouldn't stop running, Justin knew that to stop would mean death. Marines weren't taught to retreat, it was kill or be killed, but nothing in the combat training courses mentioned blood-thirsty elves or maniacal holiday heroes. He was in uncharted territory.

Running through the snow would have been difficult on a good day, but with the events of the evening, it was impossible to keep going.

Pitts stopped in his tracks. He leaned forward, chest heaving as he struggled to breathe.

Overhead, bells jingled. Pitts looked in the frosty night sky and couldn't believe what he saw. Just above the trees, eight headless reindeer flying through the sky, their legs moving as if they were running through the air, pulling a giant sleigh behind them.

Santa had arrived with the rest of his demonic helpers.

Justin thought he looked pissed.

He ran deeper into the trees. He wanted no part of that jolly mother fucker. Keeping his eyes on the sleigh, Pitts was distracted and ran into a Christmas tree. His feet left the ground, the momentum propelling him forward until he crashed into the snow beneath him where he held his face and writhed in pain. The collision with the large tree branch broke his nose, and gouts of blood poured out and ran between his fingers. At least his shirt had already been drenched in blood and he needn't worry about ruining it any further.

"Hohoho, that was some funny shit right there, Justin," Santa said. His jovial laugh at odds with the situation at hand.

Santa pulled the reins of the sleigh hard, and to the left. The headless reindeer did a 180 in the sky and took a hard angle toward the ground. The sleigh touched down, and the reindeer halted, kicking a cloud of snow in the air. The reindeer carried with them the stench of the grave. Rotting meat hung from bone, peeling off in strips. Small patches of sporadic tufts of fur all that remained of their once beautiful coats, exposing the gray, rotted flesh underneath.

Santa and the rest of the elves hopped out of the sleigh.

"You put up quite the fight, my dear boy," Santa said. "It's been decades since anyone has killed one of my elves."

Pitts stood up, blood pouring from his nose, and watched Santa walk around the back of the sleigh. When he returned, Pitts noted the giant red sack he brought with him.

"Presents?" he asked Santa.

"Not for you," Santa said, rubbing his belly. Cookie crumbs littered his long, white beard.

"What do you want?"

"Sometimes, Justin, punishing the bad boys can be more gratifying than rewarding the good ones. But you know all about punishing the bad ones, right Corporal Pitts?"

Pitts did, but he wouldn't admit it. "Listen, Santa…or whoever the fuck you are, we did shit, things I'm not proud of. I wish I could take it back, but that's not how it works. War isn't black and white. You sit by and watch people plant bombs in the road. Watch people snipe your friends while they're standing on the road taking a fucking leak and tell me you don't do some fucked up shit to the people responsible. I never did anything to anyone who didn't have it coming. There is no innocent blood on my hands. You don't have to do this."

"The blood on my hand's isn't from the innocent either, Justin. And you are far from innocent, my dear boy," Santa said.

Pitts watched as Santa reached into the sack. He grabbed something with both hands, struggling to pull it free. Slowly, a large, red and white striped pole emerged from the sack. The thing was humongous. No way such a thing could have fit in there. Then again, he was fighting for his life against a killer, magical Santa and his murderous mutant elves, so who the fuck was he to say what could and couldn't happen.

"I checked my list twice, Justin. You're on the wrong one this year," Santa said, grunting as he hefted the rest of the pole from the sack.

The speed at which Santa hoisted the pole over his shoulder and rushed Pitts was shocking. Pitts dove to the left, narrowly avoiding getting flattened by the pole as Santa swung downward as if playing whack a mole. The pole crashed into the ground where Justin stood moments before. Pitts stood up, clutching his chest. It still bled where the elf slashed him, and although the snow softened the blow, it hurt like a motherfucker when he dove to the ground. At least he hadn't been pancaked by the North Pole that Santa was toting around.

Pitts looked around. A horrible situation had become even more dire. The elves had formed a circle around the two men. They held giant candy canes with pointed tips. In unison, they stabbed them into the ground, lifted them up and repeated. Again and Again they stabbed the ground with their candy canes. Pitts was in the fight of his life, and to the Christmas crew, this was nothing more than a schoolyard fight.

Something hard smashed into Pitt's rib cage and knocked him sideways. The elves had distracted him, and Santa took advantage of his lapse in focus. Justin thought a few of his ribs might be broken. He was on all fours now, trying to gather himself as the cold snow stung his hands and knees. He looked up as Santa walked toward him, dragging the pole behind him.

Thump. Thump. Thump. Pitts heard the candy cane closest to him smash into the ground. The elf wielding it so close that with each strike at the ground fresh powder sprayed Pitts in the face.

"Are you ready, Justin?" Santa asked.

Pitts looked at the candy cane once more before locking eyes with Santa. "Fuck you," he spat.

Santa lifted the pole over his head once more.

With all the speed he could muster, Pitts kicked his leg at the elf nearest him. The elf doubled over and dropped the candy cane to the ground. Justin snatched the candy cane and thrusted the tip upward, driving it through Santa's lower jaw. Santa dropped the pole behind him. His lifeless knees hit the ground as his head, now skewered on the candy cane, slid further down it. Bits of skull and brain stuck to the candy cane as blood gushed from Santa's head. The large candy cane took up too much space in Santa's skull, and one of his eyeballs popped out of the socket, dangling from it by nothing more than optical nerves. Blood and brain tissue stained the snow around Santa. Kris Kringle had eaten his last cookie.

Pitts stood up and looked around at the elves. They no longer pounded the ground with their candy canes. They stood, mouths agape, silent in defeat.

Justin shivered. He had survived Santa, but what did that matter if he was going to freeze to death, anyway?

He walked over to Santa and stripped him down. The red velvet costume with its white fleece interior looked especially inviting, even with the discarded bits of brain stuck to the material. If the suit kept Santa warm, it would do the same for him. He threw the pants on over his own and slipped into the jacket. After he buttoned it, he brushed flecks of skull off his shoulder. They fell to the ground, macabre snowflakes, each one its own unique shape. He left the hat on Santa's ruined head. The candy cane pierced through it, and it would be too difficult to remove that hat.

Pitts grabbed Santa's magic sack and tossed it behind the driver seat of the sleight. He stood there for a moment before hopping in and grabbing the reins, looking over to the elves. "You guys coming or what?" he asked.

The elves picked their canes up off of the ground and piled into the back of the sleigh.

Pitts snapped the reins, and the reindeer took flight.

"Merry Christmas to all," Pitts said.

"And to all a good night!" the elves replied.

AFTERWORD

Some people will tell you I'm crazy for writing a Christmas horror book. They're right. In the time I took to write something very season specific, I could have written something else that people will seek out year round, rather than only during the holiday season.

But going in, I knew that. I don't write books to sell a ton of copies. I write them because they are in my head. And this story has been in my head for a long time. In fact, this book was something I had originally thought of before my debut, The Warrior Retreat, was even a seed in my brain. I wrote the prologue and first chapter by hand before scrapping the book and moving on.

Sometimes, even when we toss our ideas aside, they refuse to die. They fight for space in our brains, which is exactly what Sprinkles has been doing for the past 3 years. Itching at my brain with those sharp candy canes of his. The little pest refused to go away.

So I did what us writers do. I wrote.

AFTERWORD

I had a blast writing this book. While my writing isn't necessarily splatter punk, or extreme, I do believe that it contains many elements of those sub genres, just like the 80's and 90's gory horror movies I love. I went into that book with the intent of recreating the feel of those movies, I think I did a decent job at it, but that isn't for me to decide. That is up to you, dear reader. If you enjoyed the book, or if you didn't, I would greatly appreciate an honest review. It helps with discoverability.

And that ending? You might not have seen the last of Sprinkles…

JL
12/9/23

ACKNOWLEDGMENTS

As of the publication of this book, It has been just over a year since the release of my debut. Thank you to all of the readers, influencers, and authors who have supported me this past year. There are far too many to name here. If you are holding the paperback in your hand, you have Red Lagoe to thank for that. At the eleventh hour I had an issue and Red was able to turn my cover into the awesome full wrap you hold in your hands. Red also did the title page for this book, too, which came out awesome. If you've just finished the book, thank you for weathering the storm with me. Sprinkles is just getting started…

ABOUT THE AUTHOR

John Lynch is a horror author from Rhode Island. He lives at home with his Wife, children, cat, and English Bulldog. He decided early on in his career that he would be known for using the term tube steak in every book that he writes.

X x.com/johnlynchbooks

instagram.com/johnlynchbooks

BB bookbub.com/authors/john-lynch-2608700b-3091-4ba0-bedf-183bd0cd7cb1

g goodreads.com/john_lynch

a amazon.com/author/johnlynchbooks

tiktok.com/@johnlynchhorror

ALSO BY JOHN LYNCH

The Warrior Retreat

Expiration of Sentence

Woe To Those Who Dwell on Earth